DEPTH SOUNDER SECRETS

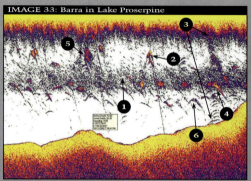
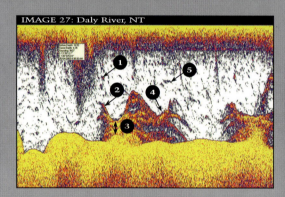

DEPTH SOUNDER SECRETS

Rick Huckstepp

First published in 2006 by
Australian Fishing Network Pty Ltd
48 Centre Way, South Croydon, VIC 3136
Telephone: (03) 9761 4044
Facsimile: (03 9761 4055
Email: sales@afn.com.au
Website: www.afn.com.au

Copyright © Rick Huckstepp
Australian Fishing Network 2006

ISBN 186513103 2

This book is copyright. Except for the purpose of fair reviewing, no part of this publication may be reproduced or transmitted in any form or by any means, electronic or mechanical, including photocopying, recording, or any information storage and retrieval system, without permission in writing from the publisher. Infringers of copyright render themselves liable to prosecution.

CONTENTS

Introduction	7
What to Look for When Buying a Depth Sounder	8
Hints for Installation of Your Depth Sounder	11
Sonar—How it Works	13
How Fish Arches are Formed	14
Fish ID	20
Sensitivity	21
Colour Line	24
Depth Range	27
Utilising More Pixels	29
Zoom	31
Chart Speed	33
Noise Filters for Surface Clarity	34
How Much Bottom am I Covering with My Transducer	35
Decyphering Screens	36
What Transducer do I Need?	50
Caring for Your Fish Finder	55

The author with a Cooktown, Far North Queensland, coral trout taken in 85 metres of water. Quality fish are often found on and near some of the smallest structure and in deep water that structure may be hard to detect. That's why they are there in the first place, no one else has found them either! Astute use of a quality depth sounder makes the task that much easier and opens up your fishing career to bigger and better successes.

INTRODUCTION

For the past decade I have attended boat shows in the States and Territories of this continent, talking marine electronics with people who have been baffled and frustrated by the science of fish finding.

Standing on stage before a sea of faces it is often quite difficult to see the facial recognition of a poor bewildered boating angler as the 'penny drops' and they finally grasp a particular point about their depth sounder that has evaded them for years. The never-ending thirst for information on this subject has resulted in myself and many others writing page after page in national and state based fishing and boating publications on this very subject.

This book is about demystifying the facts and putting into layman terms the way a depth sounder operates but more importantly what the operator should be looking for. This book has come about because of the countless times I have stepped down off stage and been approached by members of the audience begging for a publication such as this. To all those people, I hope 'Depth Sounder Secrets' fills the bill! And if you remember only one thing out of the pages of this book, let it be this; as finding fish becomes more difficult in an environment that is coming under increasing pressure from many sectors of the fishing, boating and conservation movements, you will have to be more diligent in the way you interpret what you see on the screen of your depth sounder to maintain good results in the creel or catch and release. The bottom line is—you will never stop learning. I hope this book helps you on your way, so good luck, good fishing and safe boating!

What to Look for When Buying a Depth Sounder

As we peruse the confusing array of electronics at our marine retailer, tackle shop or boat show display, we are usually the subject of bombardment with all manner of information on what 'this' does or why the other company's unit is lousy and so on. Unfortunately the latter tack comes naturally to some sales people who think it is a good pitch and all it does is raise suspicion in my mind that perhaps there is something better to look at other than what is being rammed down my throat right at that moment! In other words, the best way to promote an opposition product is to 'dump' on it or 'slag' it. We should make a cool and calm comparison of each unit's specifications and the first one we tend to be told about is **POWER** output. This is one aspect some sales people will grasp onto as a major benefit of a particular unit. Sure, power is important, but from the outset the most important aspect when buying any depth sounder or GPS is **RESOLUTION**.

RESOLUTION

Resolution is made up of a number of aspects.

PIXEL COUNT

This is a vital part of resolution and the bottom line here is that you should buy the highest pixel count screen that you can afford.

It is a fact that the screen makes up a good part of the cost of the overall unit, but simply, you get what you pay for. There are some screens on depth sounders in today's market that are absolutely woeful and the only good thing about the unit is the price!

It is the vertical pixel count that is the most important (you will see pixel counts being quoted such as 480 vertical x 240 wide) and it has a direct bearing on the overall resolution of the unit. The horizontal pixel count merely gives you more information before it falls off the end of the screen and is never seen again. Basically, a greater horizontal pixel count shows you more history of what you have just driven over in your boat.

If you were to double the amount of vertical pixels on the screen, theoretically you should be able to double the amount of information being shown to you. Having said that, often we do not utilise the screen correctly. (See chapter on Utilising More Pixels and chapter on Depth Range)

LEVELS OF COLOUR OR GRAY

There are basic fish finders on the market that exhibit screens with just a few levels of colour or gray. These units make it difficult to decipher density of signal return simply because the resulting image is bland. The higher the number of levels of colour or gray scale, the more this aspect of the unit will offer to the overall resolution of the unit. A superior screen that has a high level of colours or shades of gray will on occasions give almost a 3D effect of bottom structure to the operator.

You will see only colour screens on the pages of this book because their contrast even in print form is superior. In a couple of years colour screens will rule the entire marine depth sounder market and monochrome units will be obsolete.

BACK SCREEN COLOUR

The ability to easily decipher images as they scroll across the screen is directly related to the contrast that the unit is set on at the time. Contrast is adjustable on most fish finders and GPS units but the quality of that contrast is directly affected by the colour of the back screen. Check the unit you intend to buy to see if the images are easily detectable with the backlighting switched off.

BACKLIGHTING

There are various types of backlighting from bulb lit which tend toward the yellow colour in the spectrum to cold cathode lit which offers a crisp, clean, whiter light that makes images detectable at a glance and from a distance. If you spend a lot of your fishing time in low light conditions, you must check that the backlighting on the particular screen you are looking at will suit your purposes.

BACKLIT KEY PAD

There is nothing more frustrating than motoring in low light or darkness, sounder running, my screen nicely dimmed for safe night viewing but having to juggle a torch to see the keypad to manipulate it. Backlit keypads are a must if you fish in low light conditions or wear reading glasses.

SUNLIGHT VIEW ABILITY

If you spend a lot of time in an open boat or a cabin boat with large windows and windscreens, direct sunlight onto the screen of the sounder can have a disastrous effect on the quality of the reading. In some units it will obliterate completely. If you are about to part with hard earned cash and are doubtful as to the unit's suitability in relation to this aspect, ask the salesman to power the unit up in direct sunlight. It should be no trouble to run it off a 12-volt battery at the front of the shop.

POLAROID SUNGLASSES AND YOUR FISH FINDER

Some depth sounders lose the plot completely when the user dons his or hers Polaroid fishing glasses. Being viewable through Polaroid sunglasses is one of the most basic 'must haves' of a depth sounder or GPS but is one aspect that some units fail. Let's face it, in this day and age of eye cancers from exposure to the sun and eye damage from fish hooks, we really shouldn't be fishing without our sunnies. Take them with you when you go to buy a depth sounder or GPS and when the unit is outside in the sun, you can best judge the screen.

YOUR SOUNDER AND YOUR EYESIGHT

Okay, I'm on the wrong side of 40 and, like many of you, wear reading glasses. Hence I use only colour fish finders and GPS, which are more readily discernable without having my specs on. I detest motoring on the plane, travelling from A to B with my polaroids on my neck strap and my reading glasses on the end of my nose, switching from one set of glasses to the other, my right hand on the helm and my left trying to manipulate the menu pads. If you feel for me now, you are in the same boat. Quite simply take this on board and buy the biggest, brightest screen that you can to make that part of your boating life more simple and less frustrating.

Technology is accelerating at a rapid pace and depth sounder and GPS technology is being swept along with it. In the meantime though, high-resolution monochrome units play an important role in many boaters' lives and the images presented by some of these screens are simply brilliant.

At the time of buying your first unit or upgrading your old one, make a note to conduct a simple experiment. If you are a bottom fisher and spend much of your time at the transom of the boat and looking at the fish finder on the dashboard, measure the distance between you and it. Take that measurement to the shop and set up a colour unit that you like but perhaps perceive to be a little outside of your financial position, alongside a monochrome that is within your budget. Now walk away from both running units, the distance that you measured from your dash to your fishing position. Then, think about how much we have spent on our boat, how much we fish, how much that costs in time, fuel and missed fish and if you are not feeling faint by then, work out the price difference between the two units. I think I may have made the decision for you.

If you still can't push yourself over the line to high-resolution colour, please remember this; there is colour and there is colour. A high resolution monochrome (black and white) screen will beat a poor resolution colour screen, hands down, every time. Don't get sucked into the 'colour' race if you can't afford the sort of resolution I have talked about in a colour unit. Go for the best monochrome unit instead.

Now let's look at some of the other aspects that need to be addressed before we buy.

POWER

Power is something that we need and too much is not an issue. Like pixels, the more power you have the more the unit will ultimately cost you. However, if you are never going to use that excessive power output you have wasted some of your money. Remember, you could always use more pixels.

The power output of fish finders is measured in watts RMS or watts peak-to-peak and different brand literature will nominate their power output in one or the other. The watts peak-to-peak is a much higher value, eight times higher in fact. If you divide the watts peak to peak by eight, you will arrive at that unit's watts RMS. Conversely, multiply watts by eight to convert RMS to peak to peak. You are now ready to make comparisons.

You will need a unit with a power output to handle your commonly fished depth of water and then some. The extra power will be needed to push you over the line should the water be turbulent, dirty or noisy, in which case extra power is required to negate those factors by punching a stronger transducer signal through it. Some sales people will put 'power' on the top of the priority list when talking to you about why you should buy a particular sounder. Be wary then, because it matters not how high powered a unit is if the screen does not have the resolution or the intelligence to show you information in the first place, it may well be you are about to waste some of your hard earned money.

WATERPROOF SOUNDERS

Obviously the more waterproof the unit; the better it will perform in situations that you had not banked on. Just the fact that it will be in a humid environment necessitates it be resistant to water and in boats that are open, lots of water. After a day on the water we park the boat in the driveway and it gets a good dousing before being put to bed in the garage, which is immediately shut and locked. The water in the boat and its carpets and cushions creates a proverbial steam bath in the shed and as the sounder on the dash heats up during the day and cools at night, it may well absorb some of that moisture. A well-waterproofed unit will survive a lot longer in these conditions. This humid environment is an absolute killer for your boat, trailer and other accessories. Air-dry the rig outside before storage in the shed.

PLUGS

If your unit is disconnected and stowed in a safe place each time you finish a day on the water, ensure that the plugs in the back of the set are easily accessed and easily connected and removed so that there is the least amount of opportunity to damage and bend pins. Some plug systems are difficult to insert and remove and the possibility of pin damage is very real and subsequently expensive. Make a point of checking this, as damage such as that caused by the user trying to plug and unplug the unit will most likely not be covered by warranty.

WARRANTY

Fish finders are electronic apparatus that, like all things in this day and age, have a limited life span. Five years in the open salt air getting bashed, bumped and cooked in the sun is a pretty good innings for something that in reality is a computer, but that if it was called such, would not be taken out there in the first place. I know of some units that are still operating in their twentieth year and others that have died in a couple. Get the longest warranty you can and if you have the option to buy an extended warranty, seriously think about it. A full warranty for four years is a nice safeguard, after which, every trip is a bonus.

REVIEW

Now go back over this chapter and see the amount of time I spent on resolution. It is the most important factor when buying a new fish finder.

Hints for Installation of Your Depth Sounder

RTFM (READ THE ... MANUAL)

When you buy your depth sounder it is important to follow the advice in the owner's manual to alleviate voidance of warranty. I know, no one reads the manual and that 'no one' includes me! But at least I have told you. There really are a lot of good hints to be found in the pile of paperwork that came in your depth sounder box, so perusal of that is advisable. Many depth sounder manufacturers have manuals that can be downloaded from their website should you lose your paper version. Paper manuals tend to get lost in the boat and when located have been found swimming in bilges and other not-so-dry places making them of the same consistency as paper mache and simply unreadable.

MOUNTING THE UNIT FOR EASY VIEWING

You most likely already have a preconceived idea of where to mount your sounder. The availability of flexible mount systems such as RAM Mounts will give you an increased field of view, so consider one of these and ensure you have enough length in the power, transducer and GPS antenna cables to cope with this installation. These mounts are available in a variety of sizes and strengths for many purposes. I have been using a pair of them, one of which is shown below.

AVOIDING INTERFERENCE

Occasionally GPS and transducer signals coursing through cables may interfere with other electronics on your boat and specifically, your marine radio. Keep your GPS antenna cabling separate from the loom that carries your marine or CD/radio player and transducer cable.

POWER SUPPLY

Invariably we find ourselves adding more and more electronic components to our boats and the back of the dash or console looks like a spaghetti factory with wires going all over the place. The 'buzz bar' from which we draw power will have all sorts of devices running off it and it is common to

LEFT: A RAM Mount will give you an increased field of view

have a voltage drop in the system when an item such as a bilge pump is switched on. These surges in current can power off your unit unexpectedly and this situation is not healthy for any of the other components on your boat either. The cleanest power supply will be direct from the battery with the recommended fuse installed as close as possible to the positive (+) pole. You should then install a toggle switch close to the unit, perhaps on the console, to cut off the power from the plug when the unit is not being used.

It is a common problem that when power is present in the plug and it is not installed in the back of the headset, the dampness from within the hull after washing for stowage allows power leakage across the face of the plug, which quickly corrodes the sockets in its end, destroying the plug itself.

When routing cables, suspend them under the gunwales rather than lay them in side pockets where they will invariably get damaged.

Electrical zip ties are a boater's best assets in the tool kit. I use them for anchor release ties, rigging hooks through the eyes of live baits for marlin and a host of them find their way into my wiring looms on the boat. Your transducer cables can be suspended along the underside of an already installed wiring loom connecting your console or dash instruments to your outboard engine. Use a couple of them in a chain-like effect and this will keep the transducer cable away from possible interference coursing through the wiring loom.

Sonar—How it Works

Sonar has been around since WW11 when it was invented and used to detect submarines. It is an acronym for SOund, NAvigation and Ranging and involves the conversion of electrical pulses to high frequency sound waves, which are then transmitted in the water.

The signal is fired from the transducer at a given frequency (kHz) and the time it takes to travel through the water, bounce off an object and return to the transducer is measured and, after it has been converted back to an electrical signal, a pixel is activated on the screen. This 'bouncing' of signals gave way to sonar units being referred to as 'echo sounders'.

While the sound waves are within the sound spectrum, we are generally led to believe that fish cannot hear them. One thing is for sure—we cannot, although intermittent 'clicking' noises coming from our transducers are often detected, especially when sitting in an aluminium boat. That noise is not the signal emanating from the transducer, but the crystal within the transducer flexing as it produces the signal. Providing, all is going well, many pixels are activated and a bottom trace is drawn. Should the signal come back early due to it bouncing off fish or structure or some other object, one or more pixels will be activated somewhere on the screen, up from that bottom drawing.

Should the unit not have the ability to show the bottom drawing for one reason or another—perhaps a lack of power output or turbulence beneath the transducer—it will not have a base reference point (the bottom) to use to enable it to show those early signal returns of fish or structure. The fact is, if the unit cannot read the bottom it will usually not show you what is between the surface and the bottom because it will have no idea at what depth to place information on the depth sounder screen.

This may not be the case should you travel over an incredibly thick mass above the bottom such as a huge baitball that extends out past the extremities of the beam. In this case the unit may detect the top of the bait ball and show it as being the bottom reading. I say 'may' because I have never seen this phenomenon and I have been over huge masses of fish. I include this simply because on rare occasions it may be a possibility.

The closest that I came to experiencing this was in Copeton Dam, NSW, where what I believe to be a freshwater spring enters from the bottom of the dam. The unit read the bottom clearly and showed a weak signal halfway down that looked like another shadowy bottom reading. While the depth scale on the right hand side of the screen read 14-metres, the digital depth on the top of the screen read 8-metres, which was the depth to the top of that shadowy reading. In this case, temperature change and differing density of the two bodies of water would have been great enough for the transducer signal to detect it.

Many people claim they get superior signal returns in fresh water and in many cases that may be correct. It comes down to the density of the water and some freshwater environments may impede the signal return more than saline ones. Salinity actually speeds up transmission, but at the same time there will be refraction occurring, so effectively there will be a loss of signal return as small particles of salt absorb some of that signal on the way back to the boat.

How Fish Arches are Formed

Fish arches are the images on screen that many anglers believe are mythical. Other anglers are simply misled as to how they appear that way in the first place.

One misbelief seemingly entrenched in fishing circles is that the arch is formed as the result of the transducer signal bouncing off the air bladder of the fish that is in the beam. Some dyed-in-the-wool snapper fishos will tell you it is the shape of the hump on the head of an old man snapper. These explanations are fairy tales! Firstly, the transducer signal does bounce off air and nothing proves this better than air getting under your transducer and your screen display being interrupted or lost altogether until that air dissipates. More correctly, the gas formed in the bladder of the fish is nitrogen and this is gleaned from its blood supply. A fish that has been at a particular depth for some time may have very little nitrogen in its bladder and what gas it does carry expands as the fish rises rapidly in the water column. Boyles Law is a rule relied heavily on in diving and it relates to expansion of gas as that gas ascends in the water column (decreased pressure). Gas increases in volume as it rises from the ocean floor. This explains the stomach of a fish hanging out its mouth when pulled from the depths. The air bladder expands and has nowhere to go, so displaces the stomach itself via the mouth of the fish.

If we were to rely heavily on the air bladder detection belief, a 1000 kg shark under the transducer at the back of your boat would not show on screen. Quite simply they do not have air bladders and rely on the size and oil content of their livers to give them buoyancy. It is interesting to note that basking sharks such as the whale shark that swim slowly have massive and highly oily livers, while those sharks such as the mako and other faster predators have smaller livers that are less oily and swim fast so they do not sink to the bottom.

Perfect examples of fish arches are seen when the unit is running in simulator mode but in reality, on the water, it is often very difficult to see those perfect images in the majority of situations.

Firstly, refer to **Diagram 1**. The signal cone coming from the transducer is a generalised drawing of a single beam transducer. Some manufacturers have various multi beam transducers outputting a variety of frequencies

At the point where the fish is, draw an imaginary line across the beam parallel to the bottom. The distance between the transducer and the outer edge of the beam is longer at this point where the fish enters it than it is from the transducer to the centre of the beam. As the fish swims through the beam on a flat plane it gets closer to the signal source. When the fish first touched the edge of the beam we see one pixel activated on the screen. As it swims toward the centre of the beam the fish is getting closer to the signal source so the pixels on the screen mark upwards until the fish is in the centre of the beam. Note now, the signal is at its strongest and therefore showing as a thicker band of activated pixels. This is because the centre of the beam is the strongest part of the overall beam, provided that beam is perpendicular to the bottom. As the fish swims out of the beam it becomes increasingly distant from the signal source so the arch tapers back down. This situation applies to a fish that swims through the centre of the beam.

If this fish was to swim through to one side

DEPTH SOUNDER SECRETS

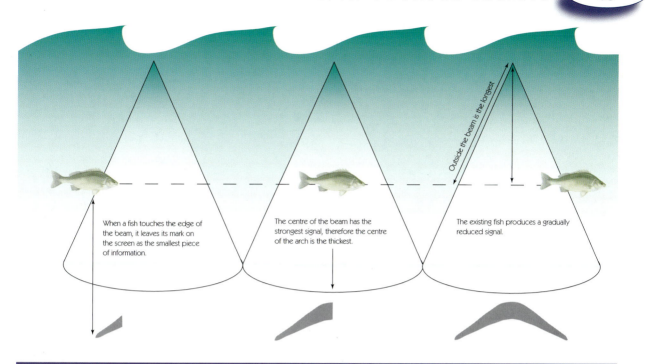

DIAGRAM 1: Fish arch formation

A single beam transducer produces an arch as it passes over a fish that goes through the centre of the beam. If the fish passes to one side of the center of the beam the arch will be flattened or appear merely as a spot.

of centre, it would be in the beam for a lesser period of time, therefore the arch would be shorter in height as well as width. The closer to the edge of the beam the fish swims, the smaller the resulting image will be on the screen. If that fish was to only just touch the edge of the beam as it travelled past, it may show up as one activated pixel such as we see when the fish in the diagram sticks its nose into the beam on entering it. The small dots on your screen when you are out on the water may well be baitfish, however they could also be large fish that are grazing the edge of the transducer beam.

This is a three-part scenario. If you believe you have the right landmarks or your GPS tells you that you are on the spot and there are small readings on the screen indicating what looks like baitfish, it may be that some other phenomenon such as a change in tide, dawn or dusk or a drop in the barometer may bring the target species right onto the spot and your hook. Those big fish, especially snapper, often lurk on the periphery of structure until the feed gong is sounded. If they sat tight on the structure all of the time their food source would be driven away and not come back.

Transducer set up also has a bearing on the end result of fish sonar readings seen on screen. Often, a transducer must be tilted with the trailing end down so that turbulence free water passes under its face. Should the trailing or tail end of the transducer be tilted up, the nose of the transducer will generate its own turbulence and the screen reading will be interrupted or lost altogether. This tail down angularity shoots the beam forward with the result that the beam print on the seabed becomes elliptical but importantly, the top of the beam becomes much longer than the back edge of the beam. Pick up a torch and shine it vertically to the floor near your feet. Now point the torch beam away from you at an angle to the floor and you will see the result; your transducer beam is no different. This has a dramatic effect in that instead of a perfect fish arch in the ideal situation, it will be a lopsided image or a portion of it, depending where that fish is in the beam—that is, in the middle or off to one side. An example of this is seen in **Diagram 2** on the following page.

This diagram shows how lopsided arches are

DEPTH SOUNDER SECRETS

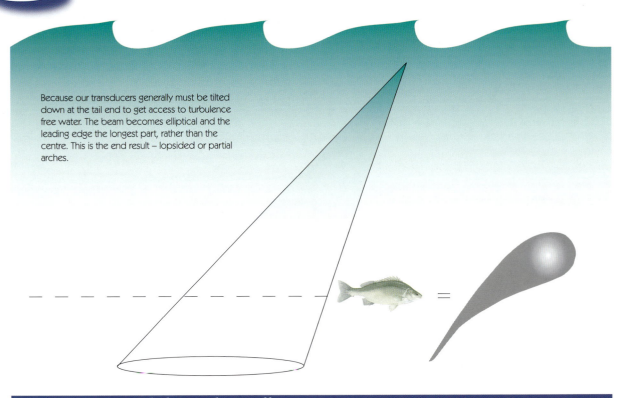

Because our transducers generally must be tilted down at the tail end to get access to turbulence free water. The beam becomes elliptical and the leading edge the longest part, rather than the centre. This is the end result – lopsided or partial arches.

DIAGRAM 2: Angled transducer effect

A single beam transducer produces an arch as it passes over a fish that goes through the centre of the beam. If the fish passes to one side of the center of the beam the arch will be flattened or appear merely as a spot.

formed. Good examples of these are seen in **Image 1** on the left side. When weight was transferred around the boat the transducer beam changes its angle relative to the bottom. Hence, we see some lopsided arches and others that are fully formed. This angularity is continually changing and even weight distribution caused by emptying fuel tanks forward and aft can alter your screen images.

Having said all of that, if a fish enters your beam and doesn't leave, it cannot be shown as an arch as it is not swimming in and out of the beam. These fish will be shown as a continuing reading, often from one side of the screen to the other. This is typically seen when anchored in still water with burley under the boat and fish come in and feed, remaining in the beam as they do so. Fish that remain in the centre of the beam may exhibit a colourline or grayline centre and those wispy strands of readings could well be, the same sized fish but perhaps they are on the outer edges of the beam.

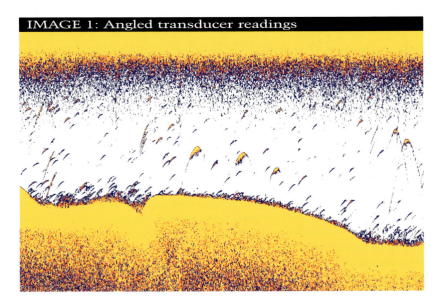

IMAGE 1: Angled transducer readings

DEPTH SOUNDER SECRETS 17

Fish that are moving up and down in the water column producing this type of reading are usually feeding.

Image 2 is a good example of this. The readings are from large mouth nannygai off Cairns and their average weight was around 5 kg. They are remaining in the transducer beam for some time. Note how fish closer to the surface return stronger signals than those deeper in the water column even though they are schooling in the same size range.

Image 3 is another good example of fish staying within the beam. If a sounder picture was ever worth a thousand words, this one is it!

1. Two jigs are released from the boat above. They are heavy metal jigs called BumpaBar Lures. They descend to the bottom to near the edge of a wreck of a large boat. (3) Even though this boat has been on the bottom since the end of WW11, superior colourline and sensitivity manipulation separates it from the bottom. (2)

4. As the lures are retrieved up from the wreck there is a double hook up and the resulting mess

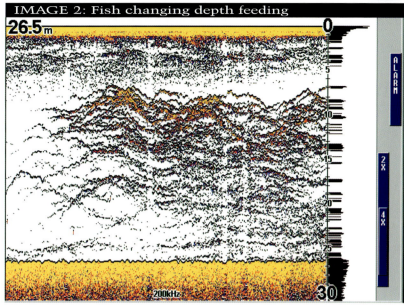

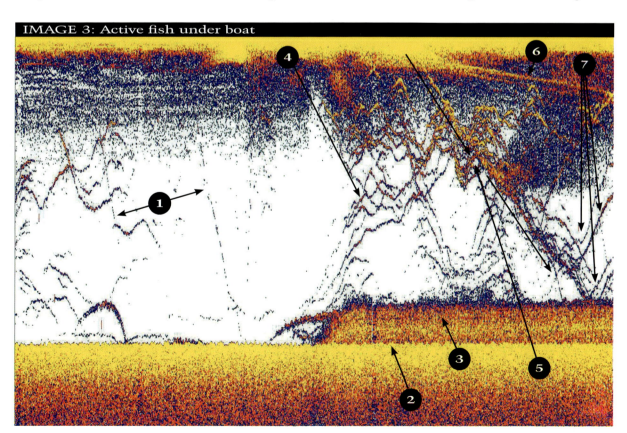

is the two hooked fish and a number of the school of nannygai following the two hooked fish to the surface.

5. Barbless hooks allow for quick release and this fish heads straight back to the bottom, taking with it many of the followers. Some of them peel off (7) and head back to the other fish at (6), that is descending at a slower pace. Obviously there is some sort of communication happening amongst the fish in the school.

Another fairy tale amongst fishing circles is 'the shape of the arch reveals the size of the fish'. In actual fact, the shape of the arch is the result of the time that a fish has spent in the beam We know from **Diagram 1** that the beam is conical therefore the bottom is the widest and it tapers to a point where it is being transmitted from the transducer. It takes longer for the fish to swim across the bottom of the beam than it does the top. So a fish swimming through the beam at 20 m will produce a long, drawn out arch and the same fish swimming through the beam at 5 m at the same speed, will have a very pointed arch. What we will see with the fish at 5 m is the signal return being stronger and in all probability it will have a colourline or grayline centre, more so than when it was at 20 m.

Gaye Silva with a yellowbelly sounded up from Glenbawn Dam.

Sometimes we see arches with long, tailing ends extending a long way down the screen similar to that seen in **Image 4**. These are fish that are generally passing through the widest part of the beam. The long tailing effect is caused by the very forward leading edge of the transducer signal detecting the fish. In this case the water is 6 m deep at the right of the screen. The transducer has detected these fish when they were about 6 m from it and as the boat approached them the distance diminishes until the boat is directly overhead and the fish is just over 3 m below the transducer. The boat passes overhead and the distance between transducer and fish is extended. These fish were yellowbelly in Glenbawn Dam, NSW and **Image 5** shows a yellowbelly caught at the time this recording was taken. These fish are definitely directly below the transduc-

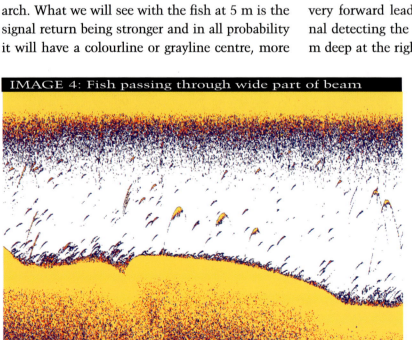

DEPTH SOUNDER SECRETS

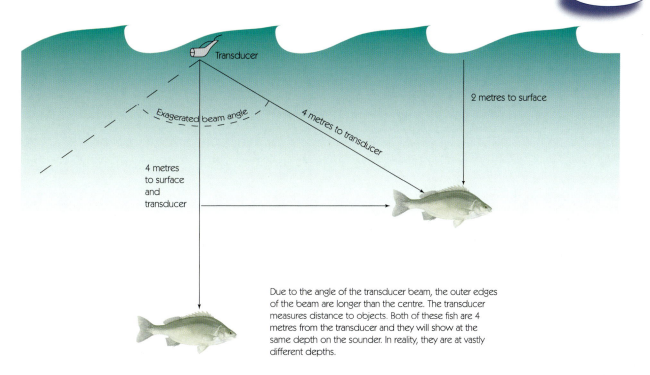

DIAGRAM 3: Effect of fishing under the boat in different parts of the beam

er but others showing as portions of arches are out on the periphery and not necessarily at the depth indicated by the sounder. Remember the beam is longer at the outside edges that at the centre.

In **Image 4** the rock and roll of a vessel changes the angle of the transducer beam relative to the bottom it is reading. This accounts for some of the arches in this image being lopsided and others to one side being fully formed. The fish showing as partial arches at a similar depth to those that have the full tailing effect may well be much more shallow in the water column than indicated by the depth graph on the sounder screen. **Diagram 3** explains this in simple terms.

Fish ID

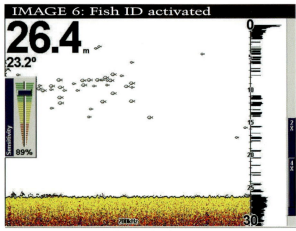

This image is recorded on a depth sounder about 8 nm off Cairns in far north Queensland. As can be seen there is no surface clutter and even though the A-Scope feature, which is the vertical bar exhibiting black horizontal lines on the right of the screen, is showing plenty of activity right through the water column, very little information is being transformed to images on the screen on which you might be able to base sound fishing decisions. This is typical of the reduction of screen information suffered when FISH ID function is activated.

The symbolised display of signal returns on the depth sounder screen as fish have cost many anglers many, many fish since the inception of that menu function.

Most units still have the ability to display fish symbols but my advice to you is to leave the FISH ID function off! The reason for leaving it off is that the technology within many depth sounders that operates this system removes a certain percentage of the information coming to the headset before it makes a decision to assign that piece of information a large, medium or small fish symbol. I believe that up to 35% of the raw information is removed when this mode is activated. While this reduction removes clutter near the surface and other sonar readings that initially seem annoying, and gives the operator a clear screen, much of that information that is removed is valuable fish finding data that one now has no access to. Take for instance the small baitfish in the middle of the transducer beam that may show as only a single or double activated pixel or for that matter the 10 kg snapper that has just grazed the edge of the beam and at best could show only as a single activated pixel. That information is lost when FISH ID function is activated. Freshwater anglers chasing thermoclines in the water column are doing so for a reason. These phenomena are habitat in their own right for many forms of aquatic life that make up the food chain, including the fish that they are targeting. Much of the thermocline will also be lost when FISH ID mode is activated.

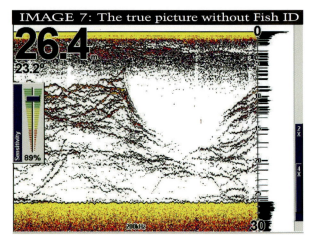

This is exactly the same **Image 6** but with the unit running in raw sonar mode (FISH ID switched off). There is a dramatic difference in the volume of information and reading into this screen—this should be your diagnosis.

There is a large school of fish staying within the transducer beam for a long period of time. They are moving up and down in the water column due to the fact there is a large predator in their vicinity. The fish showing as continuous lines are large mouth nannygai up to 5 kg and even they feel threatened by the small red speck in their midst. This reading of a few vertical red coloured pixels is at the 14-metre mark and everything in the water is getting out of its way. It indicates a strong signal return (hence the red colour) albeit small. It is in fact a single Spanish mackerel and those caught during this fishing session were over 7 kg in weight. While this 'blip' looks like the result of electrical interference, it is not. If it were, that line would be vertical down the entire screen. This fish has only just 'clipped' the edge of the transducer beam as it wreaks havoc amongst the other fish. Note that in **Image 1**, Fish ID had removed this signal return. So how can you make accurate fishing decisions on such a screen as seen in Image 1? You can't. Turn your Fish ID function off. It is as simple as that!

SENSITIVITY

Of the many menu functions in our depth sounders, sensitivity is the most underutilised, which results in a high percentage of operators getting nowhere near the optimum performance from their sounder.

Some depth sounders have a sensitivity setting scale from 0% to 100% while 1 to 10 may be on the scale of others. It never ceases to amaze me the number of people who run a depth sounder at a 50% sensitivity level simply because halfway sounds reasonable.

In reality the unit does not begin to function until that setting is pushed past the half way mark and, in some environments such as deep or turbid water, to its absolute maximum.

It is impossible to practice setting the correct sensitivity level when the unit is in simulator mode so practice makes perfect, on the water.

Increasing the sensitivity of the sounder is akin to increasing the volume of a hearing aid on a person. Increase the sensitivity of the hearing aid and the person will hear weaker or quieter noises. The higher the sensitivity, the more minute signal returns the depth sounder will receive, decipher and show on the screen.

Image 9 is the same recording as **Image 8** but with sensitivity set at 100% and the screen has blacked out. A reduction of sensitivity so that the screen clears to allow you to view the level of the water column at which you are targeting fish is required.

Finding the perfect setting for a given depth of water will eventually be done by just casting a casual eye across the screen and a quick manipulation of the sensitivity level on the keypad. In the meantime, those who are acclimatising to this function could do worse than follow these few pointers.

Adjust the sensitivity level to maximum. In water under 20 m in depth, the screen may well black out from top to bottom. Ease the sensitivity level back a small amount at a time until that blackness starts to disappear. You will be left with a screen showing sparse 'clutter', which begins

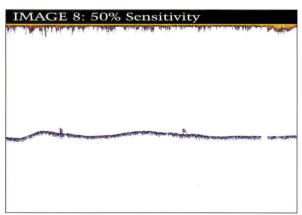

This image was recorded off Whyalla, South Australia's snapper capital. The unit is set at 50% sensitivity level and is showing very little usable information.

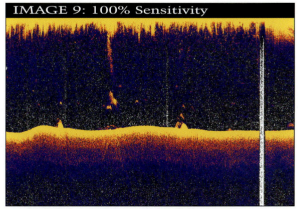

This image is the same recording as Image 3 on the left, except that the sensitivity is set at 100% and the screen has blacked out.

DEPTH SOUNDER SECRETS

IMAGE 10

John Barnett with a 10.2 kg snapper taken off the sunken holden car body at the time this recording was taken. Five other fish down to 8 kg were also caught and a number of others released during this session.

DEPTH SOUNDER SECRETS

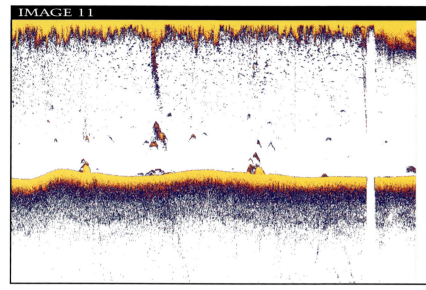

IMAGE 11

Using the same recording I have adjusted the sensitivity to 85%. You will see slight clutter extending down the screen indicating the sensitivity is high at that point but as the signal return to the transducer weakens because of the distance it has to travel, that clutter is lost. Should I travel into deeper water I must increase the sensitivity to gain the same fish finding capabilities as I have here. The arches are snapper up to 10.2 kg and the bumps on the bottom are car bodies. I know this as the chap that dumped them there 17 years ago showed me the wreck. It is actually a 1965 HD model Holden body.

disappearing from near the bottom first, clearing further up the screen the more you reduce the sensitivity level. Once that fine clutter disappears from the level of the water column that you wish to investigate, the unit is at its optimum setting for that depth. The smallest of objects such as single baitfish moving into the transducer beam will be readily detected and shown on your sounder.

Should you move into deeper water, adjust your sensitivity up, to view the bottom that was deeper than the original depth. You will have to reduce the level of sensitivity if moving into water more shallow as the screen will begin to black out.

Much of the time you will be left with a heavy clutter across the top of the screen extending down into the viewing area. It is best to put up with this or clear it using the surface clarity control in the menu, if you have such a feature, or the zoom function.

If searching for pelagic fish very close to the surface a reduced sensitivity level will clear that screen near its top. Remember, by reducing that level, the unit is basically being made deaf and will not detect and display weaker signal returns from deep in the water column or those from big fish near the surface on the very edge of the beam.

In deep water, a 100% sensitivity level may not black out the reading near the bottom. If searching for fish and structure at this depth, maintain that level of sensitivity to get the very best out of your unit.

Auto sensitivity is a function in most units that takes away the need for the operator to think. Unfortunately it will not allow the unit to perform to its optimum level in many situations. Should the unit be working over a depth of water that is very turbid due to inclement weather, the particles of suspended matter in the water will show on screen if the sensitivity is manually set high. In Auto sensitivity mode, the unit will automatically reduce the sensitivity to clear much of this clutter to give the operator a clear screen. This reduction in the sensitivity level deafens the unit and weak signal returns from deep in the water column will not be shown, nor will signal returns from perhaps large fish that might only just touch the edge of the transducer beam and therefore would have been shown as a single pixel dot on the screen.

Image 11 typifies a screen running an optimum level of sensitivity. This screen capture was recorded off Whyalla in South Australia and demonstrates how a correctly set sensitivity and colour line level will work to your advantage.

Colour Line

The colour line function in the menu of most depth sounders is usually not utilised to its fullest extent either. Colour line is the same function as 'grayline' and 'white line', the latter two descriptions synonymous with monochrome (black and white) sounder screens. They all perform the same function.

Colour line allows one to gauge the density of the bottom being travelled over by viewing the strength of the signal return. This in turn allows us to seek out the habitat for the fish we are targeting on the day. It would be pointless dropping the anchor on a flat, muddy bottom with no structure if searching for snapper. Sure, they may be there at some stage while travelling, but we need to anchor where these fish will spend most of their time. That is, over hard, shale bottom, live bottom and bottom that holds the food source they seek.

A colour line that is wider rather than narrow indicates a signal return off a harder bottom. To gauge this it is best to compare it with surrounding bottom readings in similar depths. This is because the strength of the signal return is weaker, the further through the water column it travels. A rock bottom at five metres will show a colour line with a given thickness. That same density bottom in 100 metres will show as a much thinner colour line if the sounder is not readjusted, simply because the signal must travel further in the water column and will be weaker on its return.

A dense baitball will often have a coloured centre, as will signal returns of a single large fish, provided the signal return is strong and that depends on where the fish is in the beam at the time, its depth and its size in relation to that depth.

Because the colour line function on the sounder relies on the strength of the signal return, it is directly related to and must be used in conjunction with the sensitivity level. If the sensitivity and colour line functions on the unit are working well at 20 metres and the boat runs over a very steep drop off to 100 metres, the signal returns

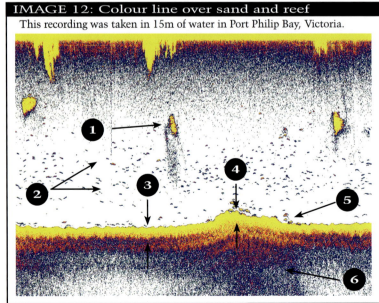

IMAGE 12: Colour line over sand and reef
This recording was taken in 15m of water in Port Philip Bay, Victoria.

1. Here we see tightly packed balls of white bait showing a strong colourline centre. At the time this was recorded, the whitebait were boiling on the surface around the boat and those boils can be seen as the yellow readings extending down from the surface below the surface clutter.
2. These individual readings, of which there are many across the screen at this level, are barracouta, attacking the whitebait.
3. The section between the arrow points is the colour line or grayline. Compare this thickness of reading with that at pointer **4**, which is a reef. You will see that the harder more prominent bottom has attracted snapper (pointer **5**), which were up to 2 kg each. Note that when your unit is set correctly and hard reef bottom is located, dark shadows form below that hard section (pointer **6**) on the screen and not below mud and sand in the vicinity.

DEPTH SOUNDER SECRETS 25

Three dozen King George whiting around this size were caught in one session at the spot where the screen recording (Image 14 on the following page) was taken. They are clearly shown on the bottom in around 24 m of water in Gulf St Vincent, South Australia.

IMAGE 13: Reef colour line

This screen was recorded over Blackbird Reef off Glenelg, South Australia.

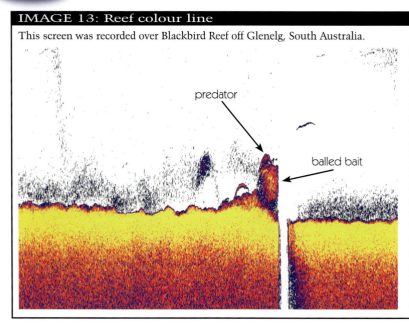

The gap in the screen recording is caused by turbulence under the transducer when reversing to position the boat for the anchor drop.

Miniscule readings of fish up off the bottom can be seen. Amongst these fish were undersized King George whiting. A predator can be seen near the big balled up bait school and another right on its apex. Note how the bait avoids the large arch. It is most likely a snapper, although we failed to land any of size on the day. Also note the changing thickness of the bottom drawing above the yellow colourline. This change in density is due to weed and soft corals on the bottom, which are easily separated from bare sand bottom with correct use of colour line and sensitivity levels. Where there is no thicker reading for the bottom drawing, the unit has detected bare sand bottom.

off the bottom and fish and structure near it will be weak if the unit is running in the manual sensitivity mode. Because those signal returns are weak, the colour line feature cannot fully show the bottom density or the density of structure and that of fish around it.

A correctly set colour line also allows us to see what is sitting on the bottom that does not actually form part of it. The colour line will separate weed sitting on the bottom and show it as a thicker black line for the bottom drawing and a layer of silt will also show this way. Fish sitting hard on the bottom, such as whiting and flathead, will often be shown this way until they lift off, at which time they may be shown as an arch or part of an arch. If it is hard structure that is not part of the bottom but sitting on it, such as a wreck or artificial reef, colour line will separate the two provided the depth sounder has the intelligence and resolution to display it as such.

IMAGE 14: Whiting over reef

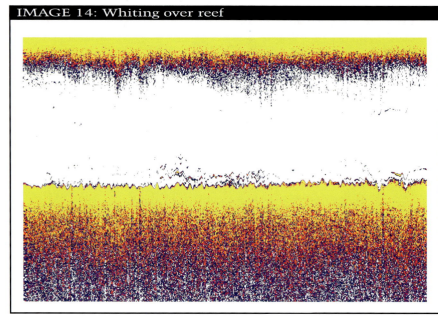

When I am running workshops in southern States, one of the most commonly asked questions is "should I be able to see whiting on my sounder screen?" The general answer is "YES". But I have to add some provisos. You must have very high resolution in both pixel count and colour line. Not only to show the fish but show them clearly separated from the bottom as seen in this image. Plenty of power output is also required, as is the ability to utilise more pixels should the fish be in very deep water.

Depth Range

Most depth sounders and combination GPS units have a function within the menu called depth range. The depth range can be run in 'auto depth range' mode in which case the unit continually changes to meet with the requirements of depth at the time. Generally speaking, the bottom reading when 'auto depth range' is activated shows about one third of the way up from the bottom of the screen.

After you have ascertained the hardness of that bottom from the grayline or colour line results shown on screen, those pixels of the screen below the bottom drawing are wasted.

By switching off 'auto depth range' and manually manipulating it, you are able to move the bottom trace up the screen or down via the directional button.

By moving the bottom drawing to the bottom of the screen, the water column is now spread over a larger pixel count. The result is an amplified picture of the water column and you now have the ability to see smaller pieces of information, which may have been lost because of the previously lower pixel count being utilised to view the entire water column. Those smaller pieces of information may be baitfish, thermoclines deep down or even very large fish that have only just touched the edge of

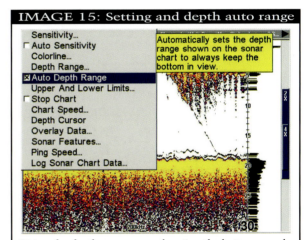

Using the depth range menu function the bottom may be shifted to the bottom of the screen.

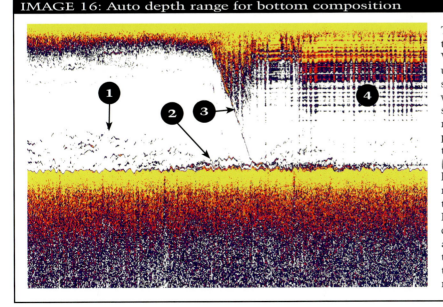

This screen was recorded near the Grange Tyre Reef in Gulf St Vincent, South Australia. The unit is in auto depth range and showing the bottom almost half way up from the bottom of the screen. Once I have ascertained my position and the bottom composition, all those pixels below the bottom reading are wasted. (1) The small readings in the left half of the image are from slimey mackerel off the bottom and (2) those hugging the bottom are King George whiting. (3) The line coming down from the surface is a burley pot, which is tied off to the handrail on the boat, and (4) the sounder continues to read the rope tied to the pot.

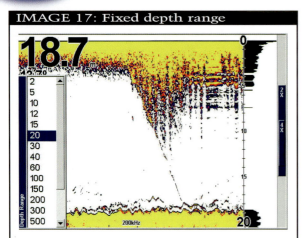

Now we are utilising a lot more pixels for the given depth of the water column, thereby increasing our resolution.

the beam. Remember that a fish deep down or one right on the edge of the beam might not return a signal strong enough to have it shown as just one pixel in auto depth range mode but by using all the pixels on the screen of the unit to show the entire water column, it may be displayed.

This function will assist those who do not have some feature, other than zoom, for maximising the pixel count for a given depth of water. Remember that with this function set to manual, it will automatically show the screen in that depth setting and if you forget to check and return it to its normal setting, the next time you put the boat on the water you may wonder why you are not getting any bottom reading in shallow water.

Utilising More Pixels
WHY NOT? YOU'VE ALREADY PAID FOR THEM.

Some sounders have within their menu a function that allows cross sections of the water column to be expanded over the entire screen, thereby utilising more pixels for that area of water. The end result is a greatly enhanced resolution and more precise magnification of what is below the boat. The reason this type of function is used less frequently than it should is that the 'zoom' feature is usually, more easily accessed with its specific buttons on the keypad of the unit rather than inside a menu.

When zoom is activated, the operator will notice that structure and other habitat on the bottom is compressed in from the sides and seemingly elongated. This effect is typical of what happens when other forms of pixel enhancement are used although to a lesser extent than with zoom. This 'elongating' effect turns a mediocre bottom structure such as a round bommie into a sharp pinnacle, therefore perhaps leading us to make a decision to fish a piece of bottom that may not be as productive as one elsewhere. In any case, the maximum zoom is usually 4-power and the zoom is locked onto the bottom, whereas some other pixel enhancing features allow us to look at various sections of the water column, be they near the surface, mid water column or on the bottom.

This is an easy to follow analogy of what this function will do for you. With the unit set in auto range mode it will track the bottom and show that bottom, on average, about a third of the way up from the bottom of the screen. Once we have used our grayline/whiteline/colour line to ascertain bottom hardness, those pixels below the bottom line drawing are wasted. Switching off the auto range control and reverting to manual range setting we can now shift the bottom reading to the bottom of the screen, allowing the entire water column to be displayed over the entire screen. Now perhaps we are bobbing around in 60-metres of water. Every

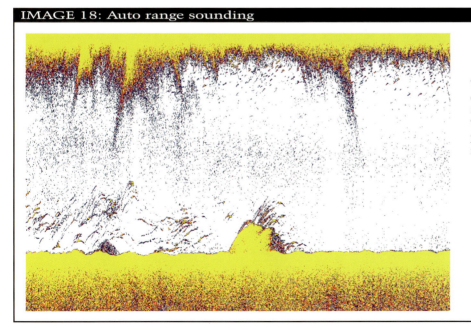

IMAGE 18: Auto range sounding

This screen was recorded over 'The Barges' at Port Stanvac, South Australia. The fish are small snapper, 'couta and slimey mackerel.

DEPTH SOUNDER SECRETS

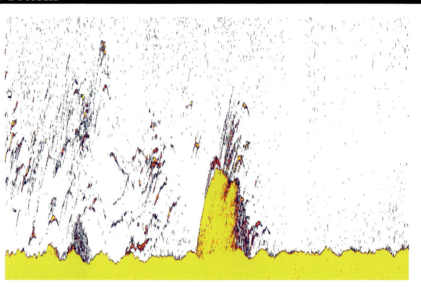

IMAGE 19: Range set to bottom

I have removed some of the signal return below the bottom drawing and a lot of the top. The resulting slice of the water column is now expanded over the entire screen to make use of wasted pixels to give better resolution and a greatly expanded picture of that section of the water column.
Note that the elongating effect from using a pixel enhancing function in this situation is a lesser extent than when using zoom.

metre of water is now represented by eight pixels on the screen. Utilising such a pixel enhancement feature we can pick out say a 10-metre segment of the water column and expand it over the entire screen. When this is done, every metre of water will now be represented by 48 pixels. You are now starting to get the big picture—literally!

Objects such as fish, weed and structure that could not be seen due to their small size relative to the full water column shown on screen may become visible when this function is utilised.

Used effectively this allows one to fish in say 100 metres of water and view perhaps only the bottom 3 metres. This expansion of the picture is a boon to those looking for corals and other 'live' bottom attempting to detect fish in that habitat.

This function may be used to view a level in the water above the bottom such as that occupied by a thermocline. Provided the unit is capable of it, the entire thermocline may be displayed over the entire screen. This is deadly technology to the avid bass fisher who can use it to expand various layers of water in search of his or her quarry.

Having set our sensitivity high so that we can see those thermoclines easily, the top part of our screen often blacks out and appears cluttered. By utilising the zoom or other pixel enhancing feature on the unit, we can effectively remove that surface clutter which leaves the area below easy to decipher at a glance.

Zoom

This is a quick and easy function to amplify the screen to make those readings on it more readily visible. The Zoom function keys are usually found on the keypad of most units and therefore are used more often than other menu functions offering a similar result using a pixel amplification feature. The Zoom feature distorts to some extent the images we see on the screen. They become compressed in from the sides and elongated upwards, but providing one realises that this is a normal phenomenon when using Zoom, one will not be tricked into relying on those images as we see them displayed.

Zoom will allow you to amplify in size targets on the bottom and within the range up from the bottom that you dictate to the unit. It will not allow you to select a slice of the water column above the bottom to investigate. (See section 'Utilising More Pixels') You may have a feature on your unit that will allow you to do the latter, by selecting an upper and lower limit and activating only that

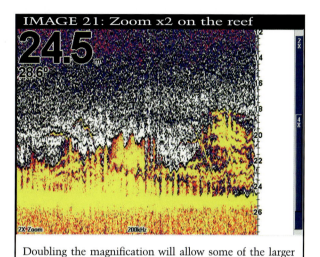

Doubling the magnification will allow some of the larger fish just above the wreck to be targeted.

section of water between those limits over the entire screen.

When searching for new fishing grounds it is wise to run your sounder screen covering the full water column and use the split screen capability if that is a function in your unit. Splitting the screen and zooming one half only, leaving the other half of the screen covering the full water column will give you the best of both worlds. The reason we

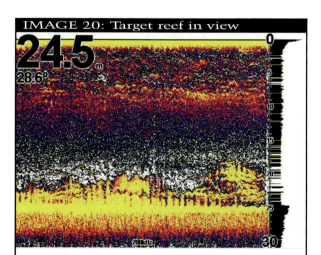

This is a wreck in about 25 metres of water off Cairns. The bottom is strewn with timber and steel from an old sugar barge and it is extensively decayed with a lot of marine growth attached. The water column above it is cluttered heavily with large and small fish, including nannygai and various mackerel. To view this wreck with less clutter, pushing the zoom button will bring you in.

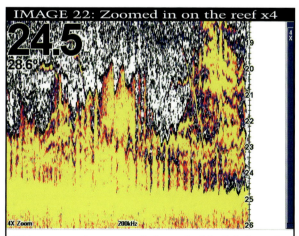

Using zoom x 4 we now exclude much of the fish above the wreck so that we may concentrate on the bottom species which were large cod, coral trout, large and small nannygai and red Emperor.

DEPTH SOUNDER SECRETS

IMAGE 23: Effects of speed on sounding

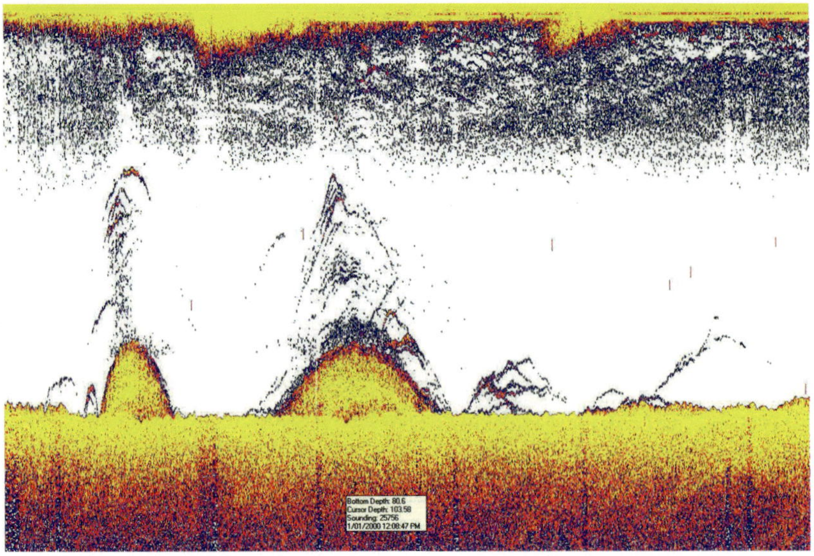

Two views of the same feature at different speeds show how alert the boat driver must be. The first was taken at 15 km/hr and registers as a narrow blip and may be missed by the operator. The second at 4 km/hr allows your recognition skills to work better.

should utilise half of the screen for the full water column is to ensure that structure is shown as close as possible to the correct proportions relative to its surroundings and the depth of the water it is in. Another pointer for searchers of new fishing grounds; do your soundings at a slow speed. A sharp bump on the bottom showing on the sounder screen when travelling over it at 30 km/hr will turn out to be a small, gentle mound when you return on your plot trail of the GPS to have a second look. Chances are, unless you remember this, you will be most frustrated as you will never recognise it unless you go over it at speed again. Conversely, a sharp pinnacle or small wreck of perhaps a car body will show as a 'blip' on the screen at speed or possibly not show at all. Looking at **Image 23**, this wreck is off the Far North Queensland Coast and its apex is just over 3 m off the bottom. The lump on the left was the wreck that was boated over at 15 km/hr and the boat was then brought about for another pass. The lump on the right is the same wreck, which was passed over at just 4 km/hr while the screen recording continued. Imagine passing over this wreck at 60 km/hr; it might be very hard to detect on the screen, showing only as 'blip', if anything at all.

Chart Speed

I always run the chart speed on my depth sounder at its maximum. This allows the unit to allot more pixels to the signals it is receiving making for bigger and brighter images on screen. A slow chart speed allows some of the images to stay on the screen for a longer period of time before they disappear off the end but you are retarding its ability to show you all the information returning to it. Faster chart speed is vital if you are travelling at any speed from trolling to full throttle. You are covering more water and the unit should receive and display much more information. Reducing chart speed elongates fish arches and other information. Slowing the chart down to 75% of full speed will make images much more compressed width wise to the point that sharp, tailing fish arches seen at 100% chart speed will be often unrecognisable.

To get around the fact that images will not stay on the screen for a long period of time when the unit is in 100% chart speed, you should make it a habit to refer to the depth sounder screen continuously. After a while it will be second nature to you.

Look at the accompanying **Image 24**. Ignore the weird looking lines on the screen. That is not an issue with the sounder itself, rather the screen update rate creating a moire effect. While not visible to the human eye, it is to a high-resolution digital camera. The other images in this book are recorded direct to a multi media card and captured using a computer program.

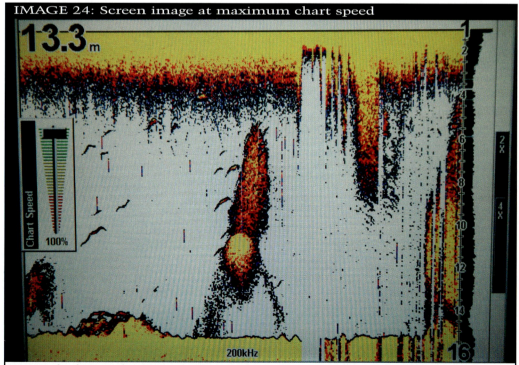

IMAGE 24: Screen image at maximum chart speed

Running the chart speed at 100% maximises the chance that a fish or feature will be captured on the screen and that it will be recognisable.

Noise Filters for Surface Clarity

Often we need to reduce clutter to look for fish close to the surface. Clutter is all of those unwanted readings of noise, which is caused by electronic interference, noise in the boat, rampant signals from other transducers on boats near by, wave action on the hull of your boat and a host of other things. Filters facilitating this removal will be called all manner of things and should be used in preference to reducing the sensitivity manually to get the same result.

Reducing sensitivity reduces our fish finding capabilities by removing or reducing a lot of those smaller readings on the screen. **Image 25** shows a screen with no surface clarity filters in operation. In **Image 26** the filter is set at its maximum and most of the noise and clutter has been removed from the upper levels of the water column. Generally, the unit reduces the sensitivity of the signal return closest to the surface while increasing it deeper in the water column to get the best result. You must remember there will be some loss of small pieces of information for those sections of the water column near the boat when using a filtering process.

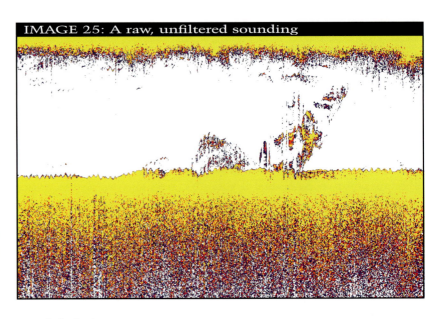
IMAGE 25: A raw, unfiltered sounding

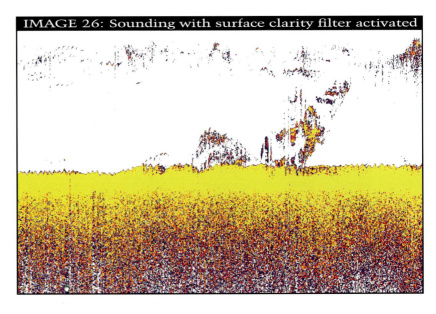
IMAGE 26: Sounding with surface clarity filter activated

How Much Bottom am I Covering with My Transducer?

Anglers often wonder just how much bottom area their transducer beam is covering as they skim across the surface of their favourite fishing spot. I wagged most of my maths lessons at school to go fishing and shooting, hence the grades weren't really flash at all and I have relied on someone else's calculations. James Hagen is a sonar engineer with a defence force background and has kindly supplied me with the information for this diagram. These figures show the bottom coverage in square metres and the diameter of the beam at each given depth.

The divisor to calculate the 20-degree transducer beam width from the depth is a nominal 2.865. So, note your depth on the screen, divide that number by 2.865 and the result will be the diameter of the beam at that depth.

I am going to refer specifically to a 20-degree beam as that is the most common in use in today's recreational depth sounder market. This coverage is only correct if the centre of the transducer is perpendicular, that is at 90-degrees, to the bottom. Once the beam is shooting outside of that angle, the imaginary bottom print of the beam on the seabed becomes elongated and it's surface area can change. Remember that this is occurring all of the time, the beam strobing across the bottom as the boat rocks from port to starboard and bow to stern.

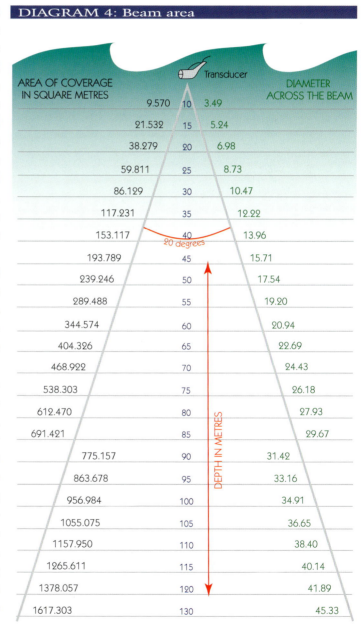

DIAGRAM 4: Beam area

AREA OF COVERAGE IN SQUARE METRES	DEPTH IN METRES	DIAMETER ACROSS THE BEAM
9.570	10	3.49
21.532	15	5.24
38.279	20	6.98
59.811	25	8.73
86.129	30	10.47
117.231	35	12.22
153.117	40	13.96
193.789	45	15.71
239.246	50	17.54
289.488	55	19.20
344.574	60	20.94
404.326	65	22.69
468.922	70	24.43
538.303	75	26.18
612.470	80	27.93
691.421	85	29.67
775.157	90	31.42
863.678	95	33.16
956.984	100	34.91
1055.075	105	36.65
1157.950	110	38.40
1265.611	115	40.14
1378.057	120	41.89
1617.303	130	45.33

Decyphering Screens

Image 27: If you first thought that this image looked like a tree lying on its side, on the bottom, you thought correctly. It is a large tree on the bottom of the Daly River, Northern Territory.

(**1**) These solid readings clearly display colour line centres and are of large fish but importantly, fish closer to the centre of the beam than seen at (**5**)

(**2**) Roots of the tree.

(**3**) Between the arrow points we detect the tree trunk. Below that the unit has detected and clearly shown a build up of silt against the trunk.

(**4**) Tree limbs and branches.

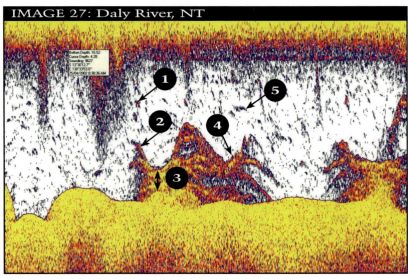

Image 28: Still in the Daly River, NT we are at the famous 'S' Bends, a place where more 20 kg-plus fish get caught during major fishing tournaments than anywhere else in this river system. Fish caught during the session that this screen was recorded measured from 87 to 109 cm in length and they were all barramundi. **Image 29** is one of those fish at 109 cm.

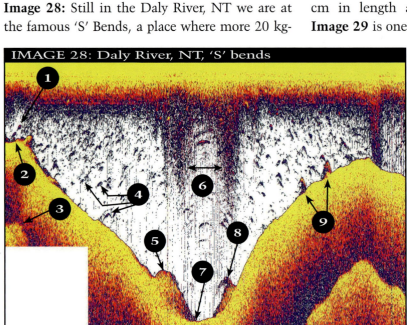

(**1**) Solid fish under the boat on the craggy top of the rock bar.

(**2**) The rock bar itself.

(**3**) The depth sounder detects a solid second echo indicating that the bottom is hard and it is in fact solid matter consisting of laterite, commonly called 'coffee rock'.

(**4**) These are all fish spread through the water column, sitting in the lea of the rock bar as the current races across the top.

(**5**) This feature has been

DEPTH SOUNDER SECRETS 37

IMAGE 29

A jump like this makes all the effort of decyphering a sounder screen worthwhile.

on the bottom side of the rock bar for years. It may be a big tree that has been covered over by mud and sand which has compacted or it may be a rocky outcrop.

(**6**) Vertical streaks like this are usually electrical interference but in this case it is interference from another transducer on a boat near by. There were in fact 17 boats fishing in close company when this image was taken, all cashing in on a hot bite.

(**7**) At this point the boat is turned around and we watch the bottom rise to the top of the rock bar.

(**8**) Here we have a huge fish sitting on that covered tree or rocky outcrop. We missed him on the downstream run and on our return we are just slightly off course, dodging oncoming boat traffic and detect him.

(**9**) Some 'thumper' fish sitting on small outcrops on the side of the sloping rock bar.

DEPTH SOUNDER SECRETS

Image 30: Thermoclines are an important feature to look for when fishing impoundments for all manner of species of fish. This is a very solid thermocline in Glenbawn Dam and there are tightly packed bait balls and singular fish within it and above it.

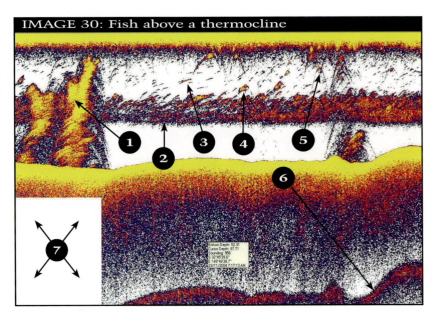

(**1**) A pair of solid trees still upright but fully submerged.

(**2**) The thermocline has a very definite bottom side. Note there are no fish below it. This could be because of water temperature or quality below that point not suiting resident fish at the time.

(**3**) A solid fish is detected on the edge of the beam.

(**4**) This fish is more central to the beam and if you look closely, it may be two fish very close together as there are two arches almost superimposed over each other. This is typical of how high resolution will help you target and separate fish signal returns.

(**5**) A long tailing arch on this fish identifies its location to be in the centre of the beam as the boat passes overhead.

(**6**) A second echo usually indicates you are over hard bottom. The unit will lose the ability to show this as the water deepens, which results in a weaker signal return.

(**7**) This blank section of the screen is from the automatic range changing, cutting in. Note that the bottom is showing on the screen about half way up and all those pixels below are totally wasted on this view.

IMAGE 31: This is at Somerset Dam, South East Queensland when the bass were hot to trot.

(**1**) A 3 kg downrigger bomb suspended from a Scotty downrigger close to the transducer location. It shows a strong signal return, much stronger than that seen at (**3**) which is the same size bomb but suspended off a downrigger that is about 2 metres further away than the first. The 'blipping' effect is caused when the boat goes side on and rocks side to side in the wind-driven chop, causing the transducer beam to strobe across the bomb.

(**2**) Here the first bomb is raised to take into account the

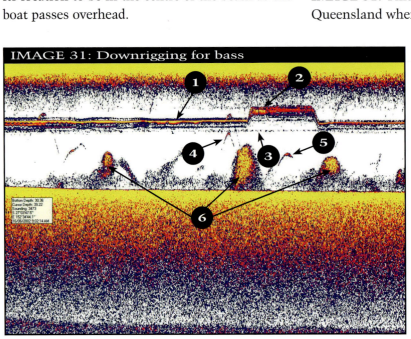

DEPTH SOUNDER SECRETS

You are entitled to a smug look when barra of this size are sounded up and caught.

diving depth of the lure behind the bomb to target the full arches caused by the fish at (4) which was obviously directly under the boat and within Scotty's range.

(5) A solid signal return from a good fish. The bass caught on the day in this session numbered 11 and the largest was 52 cm.

(6) When baitballs get tight like this it is usually because their predators have heard the 'gong' for lunchtime!

(3) This is a buoy rope near the dam wall. Note how the unit reads it as a vertical series of arches.

(4) A very solid fish return from a fish close to the buoy rope.

(5) Most of the bait, which was most likely herring, is grouped up in balls, obviously in fear for their lives.

(6) Another big fish arch from a fish closer to the outer edge of the transducer beam.

Image 33: This complicated screen was recorded in Lake Proserpine, commonly referred to as Peter Faust Dam. It was low light overcast conditions as seen in **Image 32**, which shows a typical barra, one of seven caught in this session.

(1) A strong thermocline is present half way down in the water column.

(2) Three good fish cruise together and go through the very centre of the transducer beam creating long tailing fish arches.

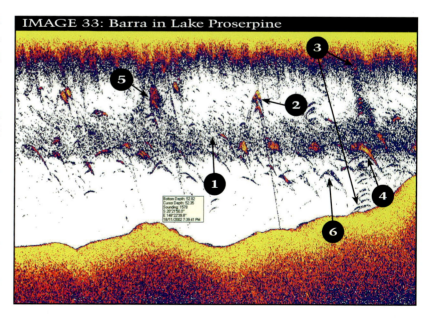

Image 34: This screen capture was over car bodies dumped offshore of Whyalla, in South Australia's Spencer Gulf. The boat is running at trolling speed over the structure below. At (**1**) we detect a solid mass of bait, most likely pilchards. The fact that the bait ball is elongated upwards indicates that they have predators to their sides. Above this main mass the pilchards are less dense but still compacted. I have turned the boat about and run over the area again.

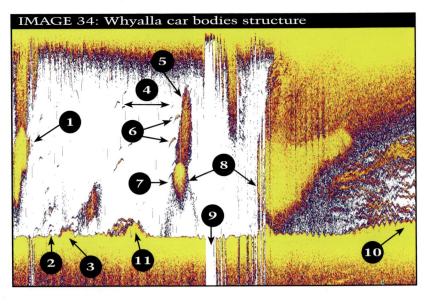

At (**2**), solid fish arches are detected next to a broken down car body (**3**) and (**11**). These fish were detected by the centre of the transducer beam and exhibit a strong signal return.

At (**4**) there are weak signal returns from fish, possibly from snapper the same size as seen at (**6**), which are detected by the outer edges of the signal.

At (**5**) we see the same bait school as at (**1**), the boat having turned about. As can be seen here the boat overhead has forced the bait down and they have further compacted, especially so at (**7**), making it easy pickings for the predators at (**6**).

At (**9**) we have lined the boat up, taking into account tide and wind, dropped the anchor and reverse thrust drags turbulence under the transducer breaking the signal return.

At (**8**) we see the same bait school as we did at (**7**) but now they remain in the beam and are continually read by the depth sounder.

At (**10**) we see the same wreck as at (**11**), also continually staying within the beam and the fish above it are showing as continuous lines.

As can be seen here, the shapes of fish arches are dependant on the speed the fish swims through the beam or the speed that the beam travels over the fish. This also has a direct bearing on how we see structure.

Damien Huckstepp with a fish taken from this 'drop'.

Image 36: In around 18 metres of water we see a broken down wreck at (**1**). Note how fish hang off these relatively small pieces of structure (**2**). Structure so small in fact, had I been using a screen with half the number of pixels (this one features 480 vertical pixels) that structure would have been half as obvious as well as the depth sounder showing diminished return from the fish.

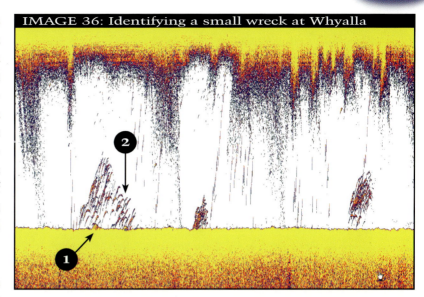

Image 37: Still at Whyalla we are passing over a snapper 'drop' that consists of a series of car bodies. At (**1**) is one that has rubbish on the bottom next to it and resident bait and bigger fish above it.

At (**2**) is an old wreck that has been down there for so long the colour line shows it as being part of the bottom. That at (**3**) is a fresh addition to the wreck, planted there three months before this image was captured. (good shot!) The colour line of the depth sounder shows clear separation of it from the older section. It also separates good fish sitting to its left on the image and others at (**4**) above it.

At (**5**) we see typical interference from other electronics on board the boat. It is intermittent across the screen.

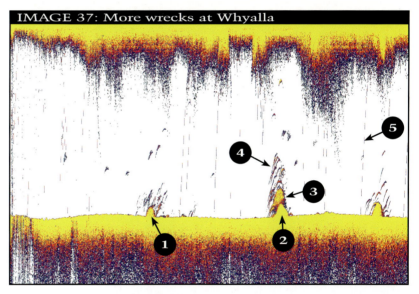

Image 38: Here we see a mass of fish, which are juvenile snapper, sitting tight on the bottom in 17 metres of water. Well above them, (**2**), single fish are hovering in the water column. At (**1**) a small Squidgy soft plastic lure with lead head descends in the water column next to the transducer. At (**3**) the fish see or hear the lure coming and rise to check it out.

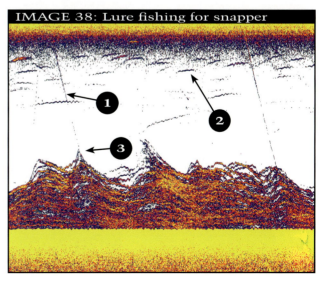

Image 39: Still in Whyalla at (**1**) we have travelled across the top of a sunken 35 foot boat. It was sunk on an old car body 'drop', the remnants of the cars are seen on the bottom next to it. At (**2**) we detect some possible live growth on the bottom, which may be weed or old ropes and other rubbish dumped there. At (**3**), the fish are stacked on top of each other.

Image 40: In 30 metres of water off Cairns, this solid wreck has plenty of inhabitants. At (**1**) we see a baited jig being lowered to fish, that are sitting tight on the bottom next to the wreck at (**3**). Having been down there probably since the end of WW11, the wreck is almost part of the bottom with a faint colourline indication at (**5**), telling us that it is artificial to the area.

Once we start jigging, the fish rise off the bottom (**2**) when the feed 'gong' sounds.

With some feeding activity, frenzy is triggered and the fish ball up over the top of the wreck chasing a meal (**4**).

Image 41: This busy screen capture will have the average fisho drooling at the mouth! Again in Far North Queensland, we see at (**1**) the true bottom. At (**2**) the top of hard structure is seen. It is a solid wreck that has been on the bottom since the end of WW11. Between the points at (**3**) we see there are thick masses of weed growing on this wreck. At (**4**), we see solid readings of big fish trolling the waters between the wreck and the surface. A number of trevally were caught and released here by Tim Staudinger of Bumpa-Bar lures.

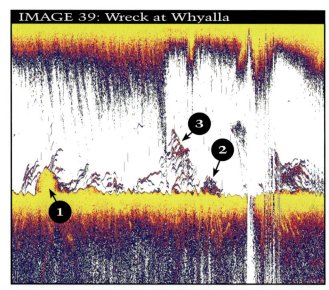

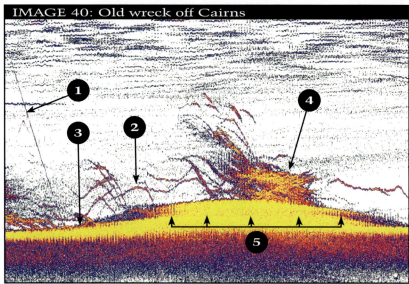

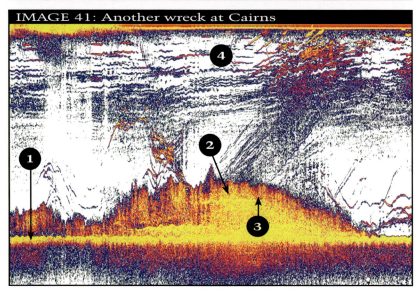

DEPTH SOUNDER SECRETS

IMAGE 42

ABOVE AND BELOW: Tim Staudinger of BumpaBar lures with one of the residents of a wreck site in far north Queensland.

IMAGE 43

DEPTH SOUNDER SECRETS

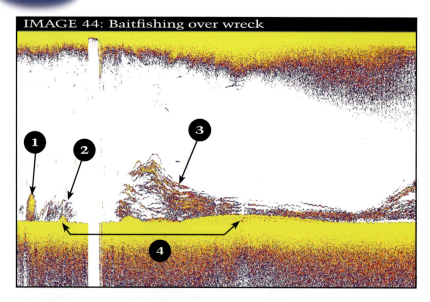

IMAGE 44: Baitfishing over wreck

Image 44: Navigating to a waypoint we cross over a bait ball at (**1**) which is sitting with small fish, most likely snapper at (**2**), near a wreck (**4**). This is the same wreck as seen in the middle of the screen at (**4**) and once bait is dropped down we attract more fish as seen at (**3**). Now both wreck and fish stay in the beam for an extended period of time and are read continuously.

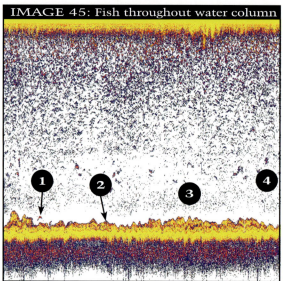

IMAGE 45: Fish throughout water column

Image 45: Many depth sounder operators seeing this screen would reduce sensitivity to clear up the mess. That 'mess' is fish, from the surface to the bottom, which is 19 metres below the boat. At (**1**) we see a solid fish arch and in **image 47** we see some of the fish that were caught on this drop on the day. The wreck is at (**2**) and at (**3**) we have a lot of bait suspended over that wreck. At (**4**) we see stronger signal returns from fish that could possibly be trevally and from there upwards the water is teeming with fish. Note that signal returns from fish in the more shallow parts of the water column will be stronger and show as larger fish returns, even though these fish might all be the same size from the surface down to the top of the wreck.

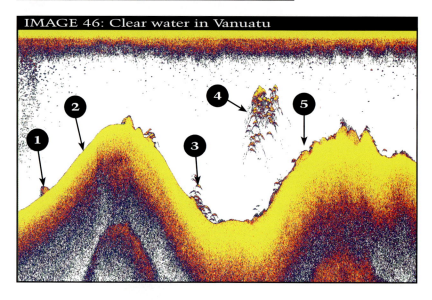

IMAGE 46: Clear water in Vanuatu

Image 46: Have 'sounder will travel'. To get some of the images seen in this book I carry my depth sounder with me and on this occasion it is operating in Havannah Harbour, Vanuatu. Utilising a suction cup transducer and a power pack we are cruising over a volcanic rock bottom in about 8 metres of gin clear water. Sensitivity is set at 95%, which is high for this depth of water but the lack of suspended matter in the

DEPTH SOUNDER SECRETS

water gives us minimal clutter in the circumstances. At (**1**) we see a brain coral, visible from the boat, attached to the bottom. At (**2**) we see absolute rock with no marine growth on it whatsoever.

At (**3**) we have a school of wrasse type fish suspended over some live bottom and at (**4**) a school of trevally is hovering in the updraft of the current as it sweeps over the bommies. The full tailing arches indicate that the fish were in the centre of the beam when the boat passed overhead. (**5**) typifies dense, live bottom that is made up of weeds and soft sponge like corals.

IMAGE 47: Fish caught around the Image 45 sounding

Image 48: Still in the South Pacific and in 6 metres of water the boat has travelled over an abyss and over a large bommie. At (**1**) we see reef fish hugging the bottom with near vertical walls around them to protect their sides. It is important that your depth sound has the ability to give you good separation of fish from structure, as seen here.

At (**2**) we have a bait ball fairly compacted indicating that the bait is feeling under threat. At (**3**), a lone fish sits on top of a pinnacle of the bommie. This is typical of coral trout behaviour as they protect their 'patch'. At (**4**) we see strong signal returns from fish that are harassing a school of bait.

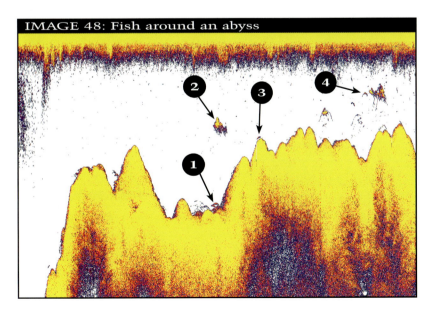

IMAGE 48: Fish around an abyss

Image 49: Often, when our unit is running with sensitivity set high and we are over a hard bottom, a second echo appears on the screen. This second echo is seen at (**1**). You will note that the distance between the arrows at (**2**) is the same distance as between the arrows at (**3**). This occurs due to the fact that when the signal leaves the transducer, the time it takes to bounce off the bottom and return is measured. Should the bottom be made up of hard material such as rock

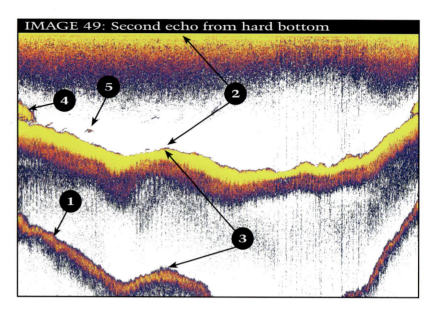

or compacted sand that signal when it returns to the boat is still strong and some of it bounces off the surface and returns to the bottom again for a second bounce. Now the time away from the transducer is double that of the first echo and we get this second reading, equidistant from the first. Soft bottoms of mud and silt or that covered by mats of weed and marine growth fail to return as strong a signal so the chances of the second echo are diminished. Often too, the second echo is outside the range set on your sounder screen so you will not see it. You may do so by adjusting the depth range setting and moving the true bottom reading up the screen to see if the second echo is present below it.

This is another method of detecting hard bottom other than by the use of colour line or grey/white line. At (**4**), a large bait school is present and at (**5**) we note a pair of fish.

Image 50: This image was recorded near the Continental Shelf off Bermagui, New South Wales. At (**1**) we have a massive bait school, which might well be pilchards. It extends from the surface to the bottom and at its lowest point it is around 190 metres deep. At (**2**) the depth is 204 metres and at (**3**) we see some sort of structure or tightly packed school of fish. At this point it is 225 m deep. Using a 1 kW transducer the return signal is very strong,

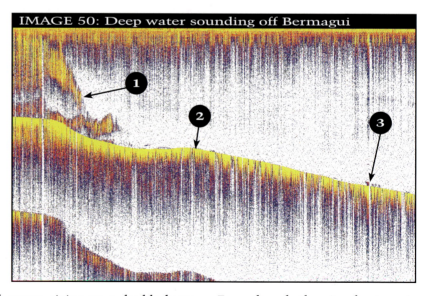

evidenced by the second signal return giving us a double bottom. Even though the signal return is strong, it is laced with interference caused by a turbulent surface. Note that the true bottom is being read half way up the screen, wasting all those pixels below the bottom drawing and reducing by 50% our ability to see smaller readings. Shifting the bottom reading to the bottom of the screen using the depth range control of your sounder will give you a greatly enhanced resolution.

Image 51: Life as a baitfish would be tough! This screen was captured out of Townsville in Far North Queensland. The fish in the bait ball at (**4**) are in trouble to say the least. It is very tightly packed as can be seen by the solid yellow centre. At (**3**) we have large fish patrolling the bottom to keep them compacted. The bottom of the ball is surrounded. At (**5**) the fish are attacking the top left side of the bait ball. You can see the smooth lines where the bait ball is trying to implode to get away from the predators, that most likely have just attacked. At (**2**) a small piece of

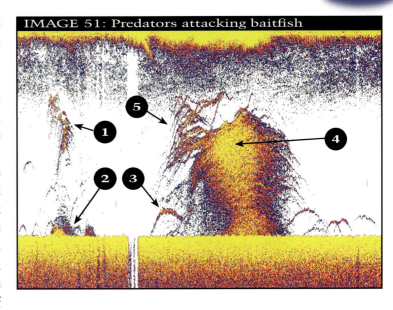

wreckage holds small fish and at (**1**) we see perfectly formed full fish arches coming from fish that no doubt are waiting for the afternoon shift on the delicacies schooling so tightly nearby.

Image 52: This busy screen capture was taken in fresh water at Somerset Dam in South East Queensland. This dam floods the Brisbane Valley and is well stocked with bass and yellowbelly. I was downrigging when this image was taken, using two downriggers with 3 kg bombs on each. At (**1**) we see the bomb on the downrigger installed closest to the transducer. It is more central in the beam therefore returns a stronger reading. At (**2**) I have lowered the bomb to take into account the baitball I am passing over (**8**) and the diving depth of the lure I am running at the time. I want to get the lure to pass on the top of the baitball, which must have predators in attendance, judging by its shape and density, although they are not seen here. At (**3**) I have had a strike and it has released the line from the bomb clip. I am retrieving the bomb to the surface. At (**4**) I have drifted off course while attending my downrigger and am now going across the surface chop. The boat rocks from side to side causing the transducer beam to strobe over the top of the bomb, giving this 'blip' effect. This downrigger is installed further away from the transducer and therefore the bomb is further towards the edge of the beam. The result is a weaker signal and one, which is intermittent.

At (**5**) I have lowered the bomb down again after securing the line to the bomb clip. Air bubbles, being dragged down with the bomb, cause this dense reading.

Fish are often curious and on this occasion the bass rise to investigate the intruder into their environment. At (**6**) you can see them leave some of their mates in the school and rise to the downrigger bomb,

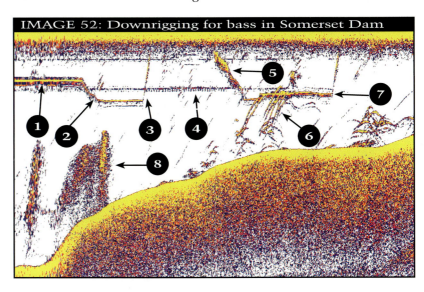

getting very close to it. The trailing lure eventually plucks one of them from the school and the line is released from the clip and the downrigger bomb is retrieved at (7).

This is a perfect example of what a high-resolution screen can do for your fishing. It is also indicative of how a sounder can be used in conjunction with other fishing tools on your boat.

Image 53: Still on Somerset Dam we are over hard bottom and are receiving a second echo at (6). At (1) I am jigging a small Squidgy soft plastic lure up and down and then retrieving it. I have been targeting the water on top of the thermocline, which is showing across the screen at (2) and have purposely lowered the lure right next to the transducer to receive the strongest possible signal. At (3), the extremely high resolution of the screen detects that there are two layers of thermocline with a short divide. At (4) I have a solid fish on top of the thermocline (time to put the Squidgy back in) and at (5) I have a fish showing a slightly weaker signal return and its long tailing ends on the arch tell me it is in the middle of the beam.

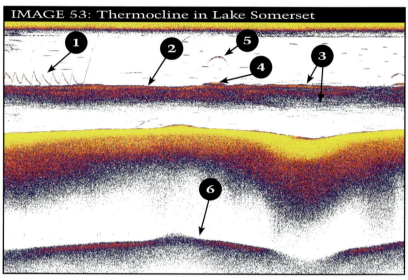

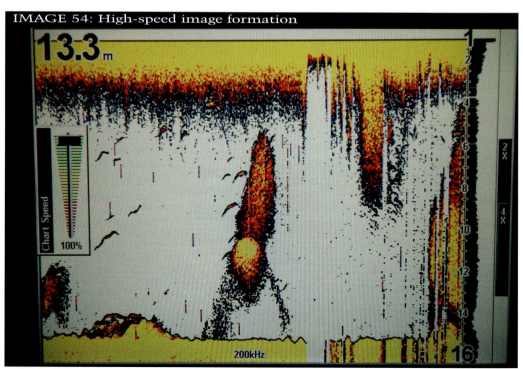

Image 54: As can be seen in this image, I am running a 100% chart speed and a lot of information is forthcoming. The fish arches near the bait school are easily visible and the baitball is full. Even the bottom reading is more concise giving a more solid and consistent signal return.

DEPTH SOUNDER SECRETS 49

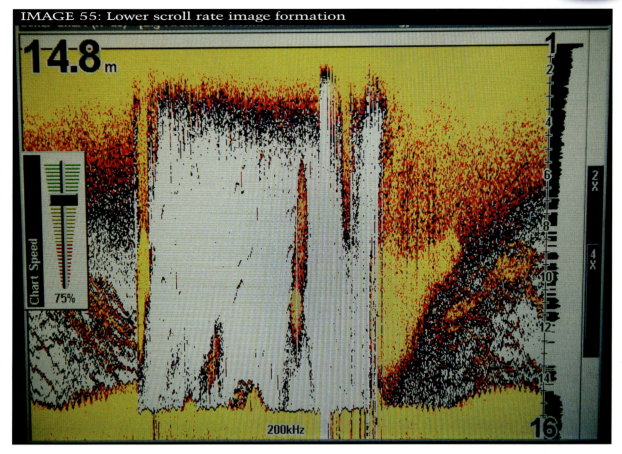

IMAGE 55: Lower scroll rate image formation

Image 55: This is the same image as **Image 54** but viewed, running a screen scroll rate of 75%. It is showing a longer history of what you have been over in your boat. In effect, it is a panoramic view but look what has happened to our fish finding ability! Sure, we can still see what is left of the arches because they were strong signal returns. Had they been smaller fish rather than the 4 kg snapper seen here, you might not see them and you would definitely NOT see any small baitfish soundings.

There is a moral to this part of the story and you have picked it in one. Run the fastest chart scrolling speed possible.

What Transducer do I Need?

The transducer is the antenna of the entire sonar system and causes us more dramas than we would ideally like. Its set-up on or in the boat is absolutely crucial to the end performance of the depth sounder.

So, what transducer should I buy?

We know that perhaps we fish in a given depth of water and might, a couple of times a year, venture wide—even into waters over the Continental Shelf. Remembering that the unit must be capable of reading the bottom to show what is between you and it, we took that into account and decided on a given power output of the sounder but now must decide on the transducer frequency.

The most common frequency for recreational boating is around 200 kHz with the second most popular being 50k Hz. Both serve a purpose but each has its own specialist field of performance.

The 200 kHz transducer gives better detail and produces superior results in shallow water and at speed than 50 kHz. The 200 kHz also has the ability to better separate targets and structure simply because it is sending down four times the amount of signal of the 50 kHz and therefore in any given situation it receives back four times more information before processing it and showing it on screen. A corollary of this is that two fish in the water will be seen as two echoes with the 200 kHz but the 50 kHz may show them as a single echo because the information returned to the unit is not refined enough to allow separation.

Water is able to readily absorb high frequency sound waves such as those emitted at 200 kHz. The 50 kHz transducer can penetrate deeper into the water column because it is less susceptible to that absorption.

It may be that you will use 200 kHz most of the time and occasionally you may use the 50 kHz. This being the case, you would be well served to purchase a duel frequency transducer, which is available in a variety of housing styles, so that you may utilise each frequency when required. Modern day units often allow you to split the sonar screen in two and show each frequency at the same time.

THRU-HULL TRANSDUCER

These transducers are usually installed on boats that require the installation forward of the rudders, propellers and keels such as with large displacement boats. A hole is drilled in the hull, a threaded stem is passed through and a large nut pulls the base of the transducer to the hull with a seal or sealant in between. When this unit is installed to one side of the keel of a V-hull boat, a fairing block is shaped to the hull and the transducer installed to keep the beam as perpendicular to the bottom as possible. Some of these transducers have housings made from plastic, brass and most recently stainless steel, the latter with a polyurethane coating that places a barrier between the metal of the transducer and the aluminium or steel of the hull that it is mated to. This barrier prevents electrolysis from setting up between the two dissimilar metals, which will destroy one or both components due to corrosion.

SHOOT-THRU HULL TRANSDUCER

A standard transom mount transducer may be glued or siliconed to the inside of some hulls so that the signal shoots through the hull material and down through the water column to the bottom and back again.

Transducers specifically designed for this task

are available and come supplied with a 'wet-box', which is itself glued to the hull and filled with a liquid. Glycerine is one of the more commonly used liquids and it is cheaper to buy it from a chemical outlet rather than from a chemist. Cheaper still is auto air-conditioner compressor mineral oil, which I have used successfully. The transducer is then installed, usually on the inside of the lid of the box and when it is bolted together the signal shoots through the liquid and then through the hull material.

If you think that a shoot-thru-hull transducer may be the best for your situation, you can experiment before incarcerating the transducer in some sort of permanent glue such as epoxy.

Firstly, the transducer will not shoot the signal through air, so any air cavities, foam sandwich between layers of fibreglass and any wood should be removed from the site where you are intending to mount it. Also, the signal will find difficulty transmitting through steel and has limited capabilities with thin gauge aluminium. This application is generally for solid fibreglass hulls.

With the boat on the water, power up the fish finder and have the transducer connected to the headset but loose in the boat. Fill a plastic bag with water and place the transducer inside. With the transducer being held so the beam is shooting perpendicularly through the hull, move the bag of water over the hull that it is solidly resting on. You should be able to derive a good installation point when viewing the screen on the sounder and that should be further investigated with the boat running at various speeds.

Another medium through which you can test shoot the signal is plasticine, which may be purchased from a craft or hobby shop. Knead the plasticine and ensure there are no air bubbles trapped inside. Remember that air bubbles encountered by the transducer beam will play havoc with your screen images. Push the plasticine onto the inside of the hull and firmly push the transducer into it. Move the two around the hull to find the best site while the boat is dead in the water and when underway.

To discount areas that will be prone to outer hull turbulence, a visual inspection while the boat is on the trailer will show if there are any terminated strakes half way along the hull, which are common on many fibreglass boats. The transducer must be positioned as far to one side of these as possible as the end of the strake creates its own turbulence, which runs under the hull and jettisons astern.

To get a unit displaying a solid screen reading, the transducer should be as close to the keel line and as close to the back of the boat as possible, as this part of the boat will be submerged most of the time compared with other areas of the hull when it is planing through chop and rough seas. The wet-box can then be glued to the inner hull with the adhesive recommended by the manufacturer.

If using epoxy resin to glue the transducer direct to the hull, it most likely will be a two-pack type, which has to be mixed by hand. Do not mix the resin by savagely beating it; rather gently stir to reduce the chance of air bubbles remaining in the resin. Make a small cardboard retainer to prevent the glue running all over the hull or even pre- glue a short piece of 100 mm PVC stormwater pipe to the hull and pour the glue into that. The transducer must now be suspended in the glue so that it shoots perpendicularly through the hull. Using a five-minute adhesive is advisable and so is making sure that you have all of the necessary props for the transducer support before mixing the glue. When two-pack glue is mixed it generates heat and when at its hottest it is at its thinnest and this is when the immersion of the transducer should take place to prevent air intake into the resin.

Another medium is silicon and you are best advised to use clear silicon similar to that used in domestic bathrooms, so that bubbles will be easily detected. Purchase it in a cartridge and rather than squeeze it out the nozzle like spaghetti, allowing air to infiltrate, cut the end of the cartridge off and deposit it in a big blob, again in a retainer to make things more tidy. Set up the props and immerse the transducer. Should the transducer require shifting at some stage, silicon is the easiest to remove rather than rock hard epoxy glue.

Take note that a percentage of power output of any unit is lost when it has to fire the signal through the hull. I have heard up to 10% is lost, so take this into account and don't buy a unit that may be borderline in its power capabilities as far as your fishing area is concerned and then shoot the signal through the hull. This reduction in capability may be enough to render the unit unsuitable for your use. Note that due to acidity in silicones, the 'shoot thru hull' application is recommended only for solid fibreglass hulls if using this suspension medium.

TRANSOM MOUNT TRANSDUCER

This is by far the most popular method of installation. The transducer is usually suppled with a bracket that allows the unit to kick up when it collides with an object in the water, reducing the chances of permanent damage. You must ensure that the tail end of the transducer is slightly tilted down if you are getting breaks in the transmission of the image to the screen. Also if this intermittent display continues, it may be that the transducer must be adjusted deeper in the water as well as being tilted down or you may simply have it in the incorrect position on the boat to begin with.

First, check there are no strakes directly in front of the transducer. The transducer should be positioned between strakes. Ensure that there are no trailer skids or boat rollers in front of the transducer as these will create wear and tear on the hull, which may result in turbulence being generated then flowing back to and under the transducer. Older aluminium boats that have riveted hulls and fibreglass boats that have damage to their gelcoat create a lot of turbulence that will upset the transducers performance.

To ascertain a good starting point, take the boat onto the water with all the normal gear aboard including the usual number of people. Have someone drive the boat at various speeds and while this is happening, carefully look over the transom of the boat. You are looking for turbulence free water which will be clean blue, green, and brown or whatever the colour of your particular waterway.

Any water that has white in it is full of bubbles and turbulence and should be avoided. After choosing a turbulence free site at least 30 cm away from the engine leg, carefully mark the transom of the boat while still planing with a laundry marker and then put the boat back on the trailer and install the transducer. It must be remembered that boats are no different to us, especially aluminium boats. They change shape with age and the correct place for the transducer today might not be the correct place tomorrow after you have hit a tree stump in the lake or a rock bar in a tidal river and dented the hull forward of the transducer.

If you are loath to drill holes into a transom, shape a piece of marine ply and paint it with marine varnish. Install the transducer on the ply and run a bead of sika-flex or something similar around the outside of the board. This should then be adhered to the transom of the boat in the best (and checked) position. Should the transducer require shifting due to unforseen events, a sharp knife inserted under the board will cut the bead releasing it from the transom.

A word of warning to aluminium hull owners. Most of the domestic silicon based products available from your hardware stores are highly acidic and will eat through boat aluminium in 12 months. Use a non-acidic adhesive such as sika-flex or if wanting to use true silicon, Consolidated Bearing Co. (CBC) has one that is blue in colour and non-acidic. I still use this product for sealing in bung bases in aluminium hulls.

There are usually slots in the transducer mount bracket. Place the transducer against the transom and use a ruler or straight edge on the bottom of the hull as seen in **Image 56**. The lower half of the transducer housing should be below the lowest part of the 'V' of the hull, in front of it. Mark the transom for the mounting screws at the bottom of the slots. Once drilled, this will allow maximum travel should you need to place the transducer deeper to overcome turbulence issues.

Placing the transducer deeper often allows water to flow over the top of the transducer as well as under. Water coming over the top creates rooster tails that spray excessive saltwater around the

DEPTH SOUNDER SECRETS

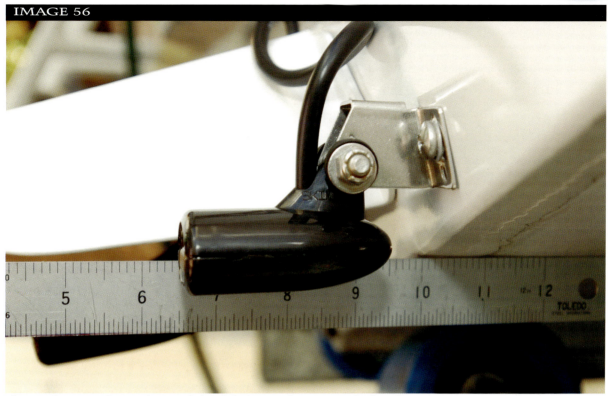

The transducer must be straight or angled slightly down at the rear to get food results.

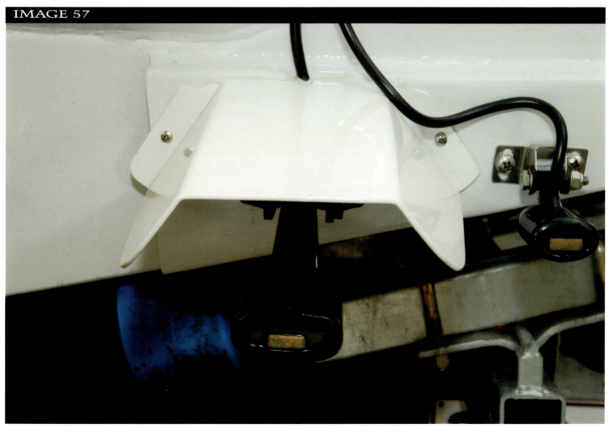

A spray guard will prevent excessive spray from transducers set deep below the hull.

power heads of outboards, some of which enters under the cowl at times. Making up a spray guard to deflect that spray is simple and a piece of bent plastic or aluminium siliconed to the hull will alleviate this problem. See **Image 57**.

PORTABLE TRANSDUCERS

Portable transducers are most commonly mounted on a suction cup or a board with multiple suction cups, which is in turn positioned across the transom of the boat or on the side of a canoe as required. They have a safety lanyard attached, which should be used and drawn tightly in the opposite direction away from the outboard motor leg to save the transducer being devoured by the propeller should it become disconnected from the hull—and it will eventually! These transducers may also be 'hose-clamped' to the housing of an electric motor and will usually perform well in this situation.

The performance of your entire unit will depend on the way the transducer is installed and maintained. While some people get extraordinary speed out of their boats without losing their screen image, some lose it at slow speed and can never seem to get it right. Quite simply there are too many variables for just as many style hulls, but if you follow the rules as I have discussed them, most of the drama should be alleviated. I have no trouble running at 72 km/hr on a flat lake and getting a break-free transmission on the screen. However, off shore when the hull is busting out of the top of waves, the hull cannot but generate its own turbulence that will inevitably disrupt the depth sounder screen. Hopefully now, it is to a minimum.

WIDE BEAM TRANSDUCERS

There are wide-angle beam transducers available today that feature multi arrays of crystals and some cover out to 90-degrees. While such a wide coverage is good for fish finding it does have a detrimental impact on how we see structure, and in fact creates a 'rounded out' effect. By this I mean that a sharp pinnacle detected, using this type of transducer can show on the screen rounded out. A sharp ledge may appear as a rounded drop off etc. When hunting specifically for habitat this result is not entirely desirable, as it does not show an accurate representation of the bottom.

ONGOING MAINTAINANCE

Boats left on moorings will quickly accumulate marine growth, which due to photosynthesis will create its own air bubbles. That and the undulating texture of slime and rough exterior of barnacles will generate turbulence, which will break continuous transmission of information from the transducer to the screen. The hull forward and aft of the shoot-thru or bolt-thru transducer should be regularly cleaned and slime gently removed from transom mount transducers. Sandpaper should not be used to remove rough surfaces on the face of the transducer and anti fouling will cause transmission problems if applied on the face of or on the hull below a mounted transducer.

I have devoted a lot of time to this segment of the publication, simply because 75% of the problems experienced by novice depth sounder users relate directly to incorrect transducer installation which is misconstrued to be electrical faults.

Caring for Your Fish Finder

FITTING AND REMOVAL

There is every chance that someone wants your depth sounder more than you do and if given the opportunity will appropriate it or put more simply, just steal it! Security of the headset is vital and if fishing regularly, the on-off routine to stow the headset safely gets fairly mundane to say the least. It is at this point we must ensure that the plugs are easily connected and disconnected to alleviate, as much as possible, damage from wear and tear. Using a non-petroleum based lubricant such as lanolin spray will go a long way towards maintaining your unit to the highest possible standard. Lanolin sprays are available at many marine outlets. A product called Lanotec is solvent free and will suit this and many other purposes around your boat. Some pressure pack lubricants may be detrimental to the rubber parts of your depth sounder plug system due to the carrier used to transport the lubricant.

Another aid to the quick removal and replacement of your unit is a bracket that eliminates the need to screw on and off the gimbal mount knobs. One is the RAM Bracket of various shapes, styles and sizes and also a Johnny Rae Bracket that allows for a ratchet swivel base to be utilised. Many marine outlets will order these in for you if they are not in stock.

CLEANING

While many of the depth sounders that we buy over the counter are waterproof, manufacturers warn against cleaning them in any way other than by using a damp soft cloth. Follow their rulebook to retain warranty status on your unit.

SCREEN CARE

One aspect of the sounder that requires fastidious attention is the care of the screen. Too much sun causes crazing such as seen on old boat windscreens and there are various old wives tales and remedies to fix this. One is fine toothpaste gently polished over the affected area and the other is Brasso, the agent used to clean brass and other similar metals. Use either of these at your own risk, not mine. There are just too many variables to look at before deciding if one thing will work and the other will not and I cannot do either from where I sit!

What I can do though is tell you how not to get a scratched screen in the first place. How many times have you been out with boating mates and there is a fair amount of salt spray around and most of it seems to land on the sounder screen making it difficult to see especially when direct sunlight falls on it. The spray dries, leaving salt sediment and one of those helpful mates decides to clean it using his fingers and wiping the salt all over the place. The result is a sounder screen that looks like a carved up ice-skating rink that continues to get worse with age.

When you buy your new depth sounder, go to a car window tinting shop and ask them for a clear film to be placed over the screen. These films are used on shop windows so that breaking glass does not fall on pedestrians as they walk past.

I ran a charter business in the Northern Territory for a decade and would regularly line up and have a clear film put in place and when it was scratched, have it removed and another put on to replace it. When you go to sell the unit and upgrade, peeling off the film will leave the screen as pristine as the day it came out of the box, enhancing your cash return.

ELECTRICS

A regular check of the electrical system will also hold you in good stead. Connections to batteries should be free from corrosion and acid build up as well as being tight, so there are no intermittent power problems. Pull the fuse holder apart and ensure the fuse and the spring that keeps it in place are free from rust. The fuse holder you get in your depth sounder box will most likely be a standard type and the springs quickly rust in a marine environment. When this happens they lose their spring and collapse, allowing the fuse to slide back and forth inside the holder causing intermittent power failure.

The performance of your electronics will be more reliable with a power supply that is more pure and less prone to fluctuation. To achieve this wire direct to the battery rather than through the buzz bar behind the dash or console. Should one of the cells in your boat battery be faulty or on the way out, that battery would cope less with power surges, such as those injected into it when the engine is cranked over and fires. Such power surges can damage your depth sounder unless the exact rated fuse is in use.

TRANSDUCER CABLE

Running your hands along the transducer cable where it is exposed will reveal if there has been any damage to the casing. Any damage detected should be cleaned and, if possible, sealed with waterproof tape or silicon. Should saltwater get into this coaxial cable it will corrode and travel its length rendering the unit faulty in no time at all.

TRANSDUCER

Chips to the transducer itself are a common problem when doing a lot of off road towing. The face of the transducer that emits the signal should be smooth and free from scratches. Should it get gouged, it could create problems with turbulence. If lightly scratched it can be carefully sanded back with fine wet and dry paper, finishing at around 1200 grit to leave a polished surface. Don't go too deep or you will intrude into the innards of the unit and render it useless.

If long hauling, especially on unsealed roads, zip tie a sock over the transducer for protection.